MW01132903

Find Her, Keep Her

A Martha's Vineyard L.♡.V.E Story

(L.O.V.E. in the USA series, #1)

by

Z.L. Arkadie

Discover the Author and other titles at
http://zuleikaarkadie.wordpress.com/

Table of Contents

CHAPTER 1

Coming On Strong

*M*y eyes ache.

Ever since Wednesday of last week, they've been stuck in two modes: weeping or sleeping.

The reason why?

Well, my best friend became engaged to my boyfriend.

Apparently it happened while he and I were on a break. But it doesn't stop there. I heard about the blissful event through Maya's, the best friend in the equation, Facebook status update. As soon as I fully absorbed the news, I typed, "You snake," cursed new technology, and slammed my laptop shut. I climbed into bed, and that's when the waterworks began.

It's a blur how I got from there to here, a quiet table for one at the Day Harbor Café in Edgartown, Massachusetts on the island of Martha's Vineyard.

Let's see…

Early yesterday morning, I rolled out of bed and slogged to my home office. After sleeping away seven consecutive days, it was time to at least check email. I wasn't recovered enough to check my voicemail and hear any voice besides the one in my head constantly moaning, why me?

Each message was more of the same.

I heard…

Call me.

What a bitch…

What a dick…

Are you alive? I'm coming over.

Your phone is off. Turn it on, and call me back.

I knocked. No answer. Are you in town?

And then there was one from the perpetrator herself. Daisy, I'm sorry you had to find out this way. We should talk, don't you think?

I deleted that one.

I decided to not open another email. I couldn't take all the "poor you" sympathy. I skimmed the senders and subjects of the remaining four hundred until I landed on one from Dusty Burrows of Golden Destinations magazine. It was a reply to an article I'd pitched over a year ago. Part of me was afraid to open it because I didn't want to suffer another rejection. But then I thought, At least it isn't pity. So I clicked on it. There, in black and white, was my justification for escaping.

I'm a travel writer, and Martha's Vineyard was one of the few islands in the United States I had never visited–for pleasure or business. It wasn't because I lacked the urge to jet out and explore it. Another island or city or majestic countryside always took precedence. Funny. I had been thinking about contacting Golden Destinations to follow up on my query before all hell broke loose. That message from Dusty Burrows was a gift from God.

> Dear Daisy,
>
> I apologize for the tardiness of my reply.
>
> We are fans of your "Stumble Through In a Taxi" series and would like to host an article of yours in next year's spring issue.
>
> We would like to offer you the feature story. Please respond ASAP so that we can discuss this further.
>
> Regards,
>
> DB

Needless to say, I accepted the offer, even if I felt a certain way about it. I had pitched the idea to them before finding a tiny amount of acclaim. I really needed the money back then. Politely declining their offer would've been nice, since they only wanted to capitalize off my budding popularity. However, I let my instincts convince me that Martha's Vineyard was where I'm supposed to be. Preliminary research revealed that the island had plenty of beaches, some with high cliffs—just in case I wanted to jump off one—and early November is still a good time of the year to visit weather-wise.

So now I'm sitting in front of a blank screen, alone at a table in a classic New England-style café. The moment the ferry docked, I wiped away my tears, put on my work cap, and decided to stop letting the image my brain had conjured of Maya and Adrian going at it like dogs in heat loop through it. I made a vow to stop trying to figure out how in the world they had time to stab me in the back and then fall deeply enough in love to become engaged. Adrian and I broke up only three months ago! And it wasn't a real breakup. We had dinner. As usual, Adrian indirectly complained that I travel too much for my job, and then he said we needed to take some time apart for a while.

Three months ago!

"You're going to stab that fork clean through the table."

I jump in my seat and look up to see who said that. He's a guy, but my eyes can hardly focus on him, especially since I'm beyond pissed off at the opposite sex.

"Right," I say and drop my fork. It clinks and bounces on the white marble.

"You came into town yesterday, didn't you?" he asks.

"What?" I'm frowning and quite irritated he's speaking to me so casually. Can't he see my broken heart through my chest?

"You came in yesterday on the four o'clock ferry. You were rolling a red suitcase. That's why I noticed you. My brother has one like it. I always tease him about it because he's a boy, but I wouldn't tease you—you being a girl and all." He's smiling.

I'm really trying to focus on the stranger, but I can't really see or hear him. There's too much clutter in my brain.

"Hey, so, I have a birthday party tonight…" He slides a business card out the pocket of his navy blue sweat pants. There's a class ring on his finger. The stone is red. The card is gray. It's in my hand. "Feel free to stop by. It's a good way to start a vacation. Are you here visiting friends or family?"

I think his eyes are hazel. I only notice them because the color is rare.

"I'm sorry?" I already forgot everything he just said, or did I ever hear him?

"Are you here visiting friends? Family? Late vacation?"

"Work," I reply dully.

His hazel eyes examine me. "Oh, so you're here alone."

Suddenly I remember how awful I look. As soon as I picked up a rental car at the shop across the street from the Steamship Authority, I drove to the gray-shingled colonial-style house I'm renting in Edgartown. I climbed into bed, swaddled myself in blankets, and continued sleeping, like I'd done for seven days at home, on the airplane from LAX to Boston Logan, in the taxi to Woods Hole—which costs an arm, a leg, and my firstborn son—and then across the Sound on the ferry. If it weren't for the birds whistling and clucking in the trees outside my bedroom window this morning, then I think I would've slept in today too. I didn't find their noises aggravating. On the contrary–their smooth songs reminded me I'm not at home and I have work to do. I forced myself to rise and shine, shower, and finally wash my straight and limp hair. After drying off, I slipped into an ankle-length, snug sweatshirt dress. At least it's red.

At the moment, my naturally wavy hair is all over the place. Normally I straighten it with a flatiron, but I lack the stamina to stand in front of a mirror for an hour to do it. My face is makeup-less, and my eyes are red and puffy. Yet even in my unsightly condition, it's clear that the stranger is getting fresh with me.

I'm finally able to see him. He's well put together. His navy blue tank top shows off his sculpted shoulders and biceps. He's not bulky but very fit. His light, ash-brown hair is tousled like one of those wannabe movie stars who sit outside of the Coffee Bean on Sunset Boulevard on Friday nights or Urth Café on Beverly Drive on Sunday mornings. He's very good-looking and seems to know it. I'm certainly not his type. One look at him reveals that he's into high heels, short skirts, tight jeans, and hair extensions.

"Wait," I say, suddenly remembering. "Didn't I see you on the dock yesterday? You met the blonde. Girlfriend?" There's a bite in my tone. He must know what I'm insinuating.

The way they had hugged and kissed equaled girlfriend. The strange chick with platinum-blond stripper hair who— despite all the open benches on the top deck of the ferry— chose to sit right next to me. I thought she might have seen me crying and wanted to make sure I didn't jump overboard. She kept glancing in my direction, but I hid my red, puffy eyes behind a pair of dark aviators. A few minutes into the crawl across Vineyard Sound, I closed my eyes and tuned her out. I didn't want human contact then, and I certainly don't want it now.

But the stranger smirks, amused. "No," he says easily. "She's not my girlfriend."

"Okay." I sigh indifferently. I'm seriously done talking to him and certainly don't believe him.

"Come to the party tonight," he insists. "You'll have fun. There's going to be a bonfire. You haven't lived until you've gone to a Vineyard bonfire."

I can't deny that I'm intrigued. That would be a nice addition to the article. "I'll think about it," I finally say while studying the card.

"Okay." He sounds hopeful. "I'm going to leave before you change your mind. By the way, I'm Belmont Lord."

What a strange name.

He extends a hand for me to shake.

"I'm Daisy." Our hands touch. An electric current races through my palm. That was so unexpected that I draw back.

"Hope to see you later, Daisy," he says, grinning.

I force myself to smile, wondering if he felt that too. He turns to leave, and I've already forgotten his name and the way he looks. The only face that fills my head is my ex-boyfriend's.

I remember Adrian sitting across from me at Babel, the newest restaurant to elbow its way onto the Sunset strip. If memory serves me correctly, then he'd barely looked at me that night. He said he needed time to figure "us" out. He said he didn't like having an absent girlfriend.

"I have a career; suddenly you're not fine with it? What the hell," I had replied, which I admit was a little harsh, especially for me, but I had already downed two glasses of chardonnay.

The young waitress with the deep regional accent and messy ponytail breaks my concentration. She sets down the egg white, country style omelet in front of me. I'm not hungry anymore, but it behooves me to not miss another meal. I force myself to bite, chew, swallow, and repeat until I've eaten a sufficient portion of my breakfast.

The best way to dull heartache is keep busy. That is what food in my belly helps me determine. I pay the bill, rise, and leave.

The house I'm renting for two weeks came complete with an empty refrigerator. Eating out for that length of time will certainly be expensive, so I decide to head to the nearest grocery store to buy food for at least the next couple of days.

The app on my cell phone says there's a Stop & Shop nearly a mile away on Main Street. I decide to walk instead of hopping on the number 13 bus. The exercise will do me good. I start up the narrow sidewalk, noting that every structure used to be a colonial-style home: the bank, the beauty salon, a law office, and even the local Dairy Queen.

However, the exercise does the opposite of what I intended. All I can think about is Adrian and the last time we had sex. Before my trip to Turks and Caicos, he knocked on my door—holding a bottle of red wine—and asked if I wanted to get drunk and naked. Of course I accepted his invitation, and we did just that. Sex and attraction was never our issue.

I've heard that writers are the worst verbal communicators on the planet. Well, we are both writers. He writes television sitcoms. Adrian could never tell me what he wanted from me and I could never guess. Once he called me while I was in Barbados, incensed that I'd missed the premiere of his new Sunday night cable show. When I told him that I had recorded it on my DVR and would watch it as soon as I returned, he grumbled that I should forget he even mentioned it. Then he abruptly ended the call and that was that. I chalked his snippiness up to the time difference and his fifteen-hour workdays. Suddenly, I'm not sure those two factors were the culprits.

As soon as I arrive at the Stop & Shop, I pull a basket from the cart area and push it through the automatic double doors. The inside looks like a typical Albertson's or Vons grocery store that we have in Southern California. The first section I go to is produce. I load up on fresh apples, pears, pomegranates, oranges, carrots, broccoli, tomatoes, kale, and salad kits.

I'm scanning the packaged legumes when I hear, "What, are you following me?" At the front of my shopping cart is the guy from the café, standing there like a towering inferno of hotness and wearing a devilish grin.

"No, I'm not," I barely say. My brain is still taking a moment to process that that was a joke.

"Don't worry, you can follow me any-damn-where you please. I prefer it that way." He's still smiling.

"That's nice," I mumble. Why me? Like I said, I'm not Mr. Type A's cup of tea. I like my men silent, mysterious, and communicatively challenged. Those are the ones who tend to like me too.

"Daisy, do you mind if I share your basket?" he asks to my surprise.

"I guess not," I say hesitantly.

I would've said no, but there's something about the way he's looking at me that makes it difficult to deny him.

He's holding up a case of beer in one hand and a big bag of tortilla chips in the other. I want to blast him for eating like a frat boy, but I keep my comment to myself. He puts both items into the basket and follows me as I push the cart toward the seafood. This is nothing short of weird.

"So, um"—I forgot his name—"do you live here?"

"Not full time," he says.

I wait for him to elaborate, but he doesn't, which leads me to believe maybe I got it wrong. He could be the communicatively challenged sort, which explains why he's hitting on me.

"What about you? Where are you from?"

"I thought I asked you first." I'm surprisingly defensive.

"No, you didn't. You asked if I lived on the Vineyard, not where do I live."

"Oh, right." I'm satisfied leaving it like that. I don't need to know where he's from and vice versa since we'll never see each other again after this encounter.

His smile deepens. "When I'm not here, I live in New York, Tribeca. Although I'm from Denver. Now it's your turn."

We're at the seafood section, and I scan the freshly packaged fish. I quickly put a package of scallops, salmon, and twenty-five-count shrimp into the basket. "I live in Santa Monica."

"You're a woman who knows what she wants," he says. When I look at him, he's observing the items in the cart.

"I used to think so," I mumble as I push the basket forward in search of bread.

"And she's cryptic," he says as if he's keeping a list.

Suddenly this feels extremely odd. I've picked up a tagalong in the form of a strange and extremely good-looking man who has me pushing around his case of beer in my basket.

"How long are you staying?" he asks.

"So far, two weeks."

"You're not sure?"

"Not this time," I mumble—again—as we arrive at the bread and baked goods aisle.

He sniffs, amused. "So what are you, a runaway bride or something? What's your story, Daisy?"

"What do you mean?" I snatch a loaf of bread off the rack, incensed by the word "bride."

The handsome stranger examines the bruised loaf as though he senses he just hit a nerve. He lifts his eyebrows. "What about eggs and milk?" I detect that he's purposely changing the subject.

"Eggs and milk?" I ask.

"You'll need them when you don't eat breakfast with me. Although I'm sure I'll be taking you to breakfast every morning. Dinner, lunch… whenever you're hungry, I'm here to feed you." He's still grinning, even though I'm showing him the opposite expression.

Really, who is this guy? He certainly is coming on strong, and yet it seems as if he's a million miles away. Since I travel a lot, I get hit on frequently. It doesn't repulse me, but I've gotten very good at politely letting men know I'm not interested. Right now, I want this guy to go away, but I also want him to stay. He's nice for sure, but more than that, he feels good. His voice, his energy, his smile, the intrigue in his eyes. He really feels good.

"My boyfriend is marrying my best friend," I blurt out unthinkingly. "That's why I feel like crap."

"Oh, I'm sorry to hear that." He sounds genuinely sympathetic.

"Me too." I avoid eye contact. Confession is supposed to be good for the soul, but I just feel worse. I push the basket. "You're right. I'll need eggs, milk, pancake mix…"

"Hey," he says softly as he takes the basket by the handle to stop my progress. "Sorry, I didn't mean to sound disingenuous."

"No, that's not it. You didn't sound 'disingenuous' at all."

We're staring into each other's eyes, and it feels as though I've known him for longer than less than an hour.

"Come to my birthday party tonight," he finally says. "It's going to be fun. You'll forget about this douche who made off with your skanky best friend."

I sniff and chuckle. Hearing it put like that makes me feel better, even if he's not a douche. However, she may be a skank. The jury has always been out on that. I shrug. "I'll try."

He crimps his eyebrows as though he's thinking very hard. "You'll need water."

When we get to the water aisle, he piles three twenty-four packs of sixteen-ounce bottles in the basket. When I tell him there's no way I can carry that back, he offers to drive me to the house.

Now I'm crimping my eyebrows. He's weighed me down on purpose. The only reason I go along with his little scheme is because I do need the water, and since all the store clerks seem to know and like him, he must be harmless.

CHAPTER 2

Persistence Pays Off

Of course pretty boy stranger drives a sporty burgundy BMW with the top down. He opens the passenger-side door and insists that I get in and make myself comfortable while he puts the groceries in the trunk. I'm not surprised by how delicious the inside of his car smells; it's a mixture of brand-new leather and vanilla. I cozy up against the soft leather seat and strap myself in.

"By the way"—he leans over as he straps himself in—"you look stunning in that dress. Very sexy, and yesterday in the black jeans and shirt too. And"—he digs into his pocket—"you left this on the table." He's holding up the gray card I left behind sort of on purpose. He's grinning as if I've been caught in the act of trying to elude him. "My name is Belmont Lord. You forgot, didn't you?"

I take the card but drop my face, embarrassed. I had no intentions of seeing him again, let alone attending his party. "Maybe."

He chuckles and winks before backing the car out of the parking space.

I'm still so embarrassed. I want to sink into my seat and disappear. For sure he's through with me now. So I give him the address to where I'm staying, believing this will certainly be the last time we'll speak because come hell or high water, I will avoid him.

"Did you rent a car?" he asks.

"A Mini Cooper," I reply, still jumpy.

"But you walked to the grocery store?"

"And to breakfast," I add. "Why drive where two feet can carry you? I'm a travel writer. It's easier to get a feel for a place if I walk."

"Ah, so she's a writer..." he says, adding to that list of details about me he's keeping.

"Yes, I am. Why did you ask?"

"If you didn't have a car, then I would be willing to chauffeur you around."

"Oh." I was not at all expecting that response. We grow silent again. "So what do you do for work?"

Belmont Lord glowers up the road as if I've touched a nerve.

"Is your job legal?" After witnessing his expression, I feel like I have to ask.

He chuckles. "What if it weren't? What if I were a criminal?" He lifts his eyebrows teasingly.

I shrug. "Then that's your business. I've consorted with criminals before." It sounds like I'm patting myself on the back for being worldly–which I am. "They make the best tour guides."

"You and criminals? I don't believe it. There's not a bad guy in the world who would be able to keep his hands off of you."

I roll my eyes. That was supposed to be flattering, but it's not.

He must've seen my reaction because he laughs. "I'm an independent contractor."

"What kind of contractor?" I ask, narrowing one eye suspiciously.

He laughs again. "Not that kind. Construction. I also do real estate development. And this summer, my brother and I ran a luxury liner from Martha's Vineyard to Boston. Actually, he started it, and I had to clean up his mess." He mumbles that last bit.

"Oh okay, that sounds slightly miserable but legal." Surprisingly, I smile at him. Goodness gracious, he's making me feel pretty good.

Belmont reaches over to squeeze my hand that's sitting on my lap. I'm expecting him to remove it, but he doesn't. Suddenly, I'm nervous again because of how natural his touch feels.

This is crazy!

He's crazy!

I'm crazy!

"Thanks for doing this for me—taking me home, that is," I say to remind him where we're supposed to be going because he turns off of Main Street and heads in the wrong direction.

"Hey, do you mind if I stop off to buy a plant?" he asks, showing me that charming smile of his.

"A plant?" I gulp.

"The nursery's right off Edgartown Vineyard Haven Road. It'll only take a second."

I hesitate. I still don't understand why he's trying to drag this out. "Okay." I sigh.

That answer seems to satisfy him. He squeezes my hand one last time before letting go to navigate the steering wheel.

The drive takes way longer than "a second," but the twisting and turning roads do help me conclude that Martha's Vineyard has a lot of colonial-style houses on it–tons of them built on just about every plot of land. Most of them are unoccupied now, but I imagine they've been occupied all summer long.

I was wrong in assuming that the island is quaint. A lot of the natives drive huge trucks. Traffic is pretty regular too. The fields of forest, which hide the spectacular beachfront homes, could make a car ride like this one feel monotonous.

"Getting an eyeful?" Belmont asks to claim my attention.

I look at him. He's still smiling. He does that a lot—smile. I think he's a happy guy, and that's great. Adrian hardly ever smiled. He complained a lot, usually about the show runner or producer, or the other writers in the writing room–and me. He used to complain that no one thought he had a girlfriend because he's always going to functions alone. There were even rumors that he's gay, which I can definitely believe. He's in great shape, and he has nice white teeth and fingernails. His cayenne-brown skin is smooth as a baby's bottom because he uses sunscreen and moisturizes every day. He looks waxed, plucked, and powdered. As Stanford says on the television show *Sex and the City*, "How can anyone that gorgeous be straight?"

"Ah, you're sad again," he says as the car comes to a stop at a sign.

"No," I reply, but I'm too jumpy for it to be true.

"Good," he says, leaving it at that.

I think he's going to hold my hand again, but instead, he opens the glove compartment and takes out a small slip of paper with a list written on it.

He makes a right into the parking lot of a plant nursery, parks, and hops out of the car. I'm not sure if he wants me to come with him until he walks around the front of the car to open my door for me. I slide out and we walk side-by-side toward the colorful flowers and robust green plants lined up in neat rows.

"What can I get for you, Belmont?" a petite, red-faced woman with a button nose and small eyes asks in the customary New England accent.

"How are you doing, Nance. Looking for this here." He uses the same regional dialect that I didn't think he had.

She scowls at the list. Whatever's written on it seems to puzzle her. "Oh, go to Oak Lanes." She hands it back to him.

"You're the best, Nance." He rewards her with that charming wink of his.

I wonder if he intends to drop me off at the house before he goes on a wild goose chase for the mysterious plants on the list.

As we walk back to the BMW, I say, "Well, good luck finding what you're looking for."

"It's right up the road. It won't take long."

I could insist that he drops me off first, but the key to being a successful travel writer is to go with spontaneous flows. I never know where they'll lead me. I'm torn between giving in to my natural curiosity and the incessant need to be alone so I can press the resume button on crying my eyes out.

The car is back on the road, passing more dry trees and foliage. I've already noticed that the thick forests lining the roadways act as woody fences. I kind of find that disconcerting. It seems residents definitely have to pay for paradise on this island.

"So where have you traveled?" Belmont asks.

I can tell he's trying to start a conversation, any old conversation. "Just about everywhere. Except here."

"No?" He sounds intrigued.

I shake my head. "No."

"There's a lot of beauty on the Vineyard. I'll take you around to see it."

"No!" I panic. "I have to get back."

He laughs. "Not now—later. But why do you want to get away from me, Daisy? I like this, hanging around you."

I sniff at how weird that sounds, mainly because I like being with him too. Strange, but I do.

"So your boyfriend made off with another girl?" Again, it sounds as though he's forcing conversation.

"Yep."

"Well, his loss."

"How do you know that? I can be aloof and unfeeling. I'm not a good girlfriend. So whatever you're trying to do here, you should really rethink it."

"You haven't been aloof and unfeeling in the last"—he looks at his expensive watch—"forty-five minutes."

"That's because you're a stranger," I mutter.

"Your name is Daisy, and you live in Santa Monica, California. You're a writer who just lost her lover and friend. If you were a stranger, then I wouldn't know any of that. If you were aloof, you wouldn't have told me any of it."

There. I saw that. The way his eyes fell to the material pulling across my breasts. He's turned on by me. Therefore I can't trust his assessment.

He turns the car down a long dirt road flanked by more dead trees with gray trunks and bare, wiry branches.

"I thought the trees would be greener." I'm deliberately changing the subject.

"They were destroyed by caterpillars back in 2007. Hundreds of acres, gone."

"So what's being done about it?" the writer in me asks.

"Last I heard, they were waiting to see if the forest recovers on its own."

"But it's been five years."

The car rolls to a stop. "You want to go for a walk through them?" he asks, which worries me. It probably shows in my eyes because he says, "I'm not a serial killer or anything. You don't have to be afraid of me, Daisy. I'll never hurt any part of you." He pauses. "I like the way you do that."

"Do what?" I squeak nervously.

"Part your lips."

I become aware of what I'm doing and close my mouth. His eyes veer down to my chest, and I see what's caught his attention. My nipples are betraying me by shoving against the

19

fabric of my dress. I instinctively cross my arms. He chuckles and starts driving again. Eventually, he stops the car after circling a red brick paved motor court.

"I'll be back," he says, watching me intensely. "Don't run off into the woods without me." He's grinning at his bad attempt at a joke.

"I won't," I reassure him. He's still ogling me. "What?" I squirm under the magnetic power of his stare.

"You're really beautiful. I've never been this close to someone as beautiful as you."

I'm moved to laugh once and very cynically. "I doubt that." I sniff. I mean, it's just another corny attempt to flatter me.

"You don't believe me?" he challenges me.

"No, I don't," I assert.

"It's true." He surprises me by taking my chin and putting a tender kiss on my parted lips. "I couldn't wait any longer."

My mouth is still open in surprise as he hurries out of the driver's seat and trots up the steps to the front porch. He turns back to grin after he knocks on the door.

I'm still stunned by what just happened. That was the softest, warmest kiss I ever had, and I can still taste him in my mouth.

I'm more confused than ever. My mind works feverishly to remember Adrian's face because all I can picture is the way Belmont stares at me. Those hazel eyes ignite a burning in my thighs. They could make my heart beat faster if I let them.

Maybe I'm subconsciously craving sexual intimacy. That could be it. I haven't had sex in three months. Adrian was satisfactory in bed. He was never as good as the guys are in the movies. It's rare that I watch films but when I do, I always notice how women moan and sigh and suck air between their teeth, writhing like they just can't take anymore. I always wonder if that could be real. Jeez. I shake my head like a rattle. Why am I even thinking this?

The driver's door opens, and he's back behind the wheel. I stare out the window at the front door of another colonial-style house covered with gray shingles.

"Got it," he says.

"Good," I reply, still too embarrassed to look at him.

"Hey, if I moved too fast with the kiss…"

"No, you didn't," I say, cutting him off.

"Ah." He chuckles. "I see."

I flick my face in his direction. My God, what sort of spell has he cast over me? I want to go into full make-out mode with this guy. "You see what?" I swallow the nervous energy that's trapped in my throat.

"I shocked you."

"Oh." I face forward. I can't stand to look at him any longer. Plus, he's right; he did shock me.

I watch as he carefully puts a brown bag in the glove compartment. I'm not stupid. It's apparent he was on a quest for marijuana. The car starts up.

"So, you're coming to my party tonight?" he asks.

There he goes with the party talk again. "Who's going to be there?"

"You don't plan on coming, do you?"

I shrug. "It depends."

"You're coming to the party, Daisy. If you don't show up by eight, I'll come get you." He lifts his eyebrows flirtatiously.

"You're pretty bossy for someone I just met an hour ago."

Belmont studies me as if he's mesmerized. "I just don't want to stop getting to know you, Daisy, that's all."

I drop my face bashfully. Could this really be happening?

I learn a little more about Belmont Lord as he drives me to the house on Water Street in Edgartown. He's lived in Telluride, Colorado; Las Vegas, Nevada; Dallas, Texas; and even Venice, California. He's traveled all over the world. We were comparing destinations when he pulled into the driveway of my rented house.

"It's cliché, but Paris is my favorite place in the world," I reveal.

"I can see it." He's watching me while wearing that naughty grin.

"You can? Why is that?" I'm eager to hear his answer.

"I can always spot the lonesome American girls walking down L'Avenue des Champs Elysées. They're wide-eyed, bushy-tailed, beautiful—and brave."

"Wow," I mutter with a catch in my throat. I love what he just said.

My skin runs hot. I need air. I push the car door open as fast as I can. I hear his door open, but I'm out and standing before he can reach me. Now we're facing each other. My heart thumps. He's at least six inches taller than I am. I feel dwarfed by him.

"I'll help you with the water," he whispers hoarsely.

I think I'm having the same effect on him that he's having on me, and he's the one making all the moves. Belmont Lord is a bold man who goes for what he wants, and I wish it didn't turn me on so much.

"Okay," I croak.

He stares at my chest, and my nipples betray me again. He catches a breath before hitting a button on the car remote to open the trunk. He's the first to step away. We unload the water and the rest of my groceries, setting them on the island in the middle of the gourmet kitchen.

"This house is pretty decent, but you'll like mine better," Belmont says as he looks around the kitchen. "I know who owns this place. How much are you paying for it?"

"Three thousand a week, I think. My travel agent found it for me," I reply, even if that was sort of an inappropriate question.

"Your travel agent? What's her name?"

I pause. "Leslie." I wonder why he wants to know.

"Leslie…?" He's waiting for me to say her last name.

"Birch."

"Leslie Birch found you a bad deal, Daisy. It's off season. You should've only paid half that price, but I can fix that for you if you like."

"No, it's too late." I sigh, thinking about the money I could recover if I say yes. I never had a guy offer to do something like that for me, not even my father.

He nods as he thinks. "The party's in Chilmark," he says abruptly. "That's where we just left. Do I have to come pick you up tonight, or are you coming on your own?"

There he goes again. "I told you I rented a car."

"And you're going to use that car to drive to my party." He grins. He's beating this subject until it bleeds.

"Yes," I answer truthfully.

"Now that's what I want to hear."

Before I can blink, he's kissing me again. He pulls me into his body, and we're kissing so deeply that moans escape my throat.

"May I?" he whispers.

I open my eyes. "May I?"

"May I touch you?" he asks.

"Touch me? Where?"

His hand slides up my waist to squeeze one of my breasts, and he pinches the nipple between two fingers. "Here," he sighs.

I suck in a sharp breath of air between my teeth. The sensation makes my thighs tingle. "Oh, there."

After a moment, Belmont comes to himself and takes a step back. "Hell, I should go. I'm sorry, Daisy. I don't know what the hell you're doing to me. This is not my usual M.O."

"It's okay," I say, still breathless. "This isn't mine either."

I'm still a little flustered after he writes his address on a notepad and informs me that any GPS should take me straight to his house. He also reminds me that if I don't show up by eight o'clock, then he's coming to get me.

One thing's for sure: he has balls. I wonder if Adrian would've gotten everything he wanted from me if he had been just as persistent.

CHAPTER 3

Kind Of Like A Party

*F*irst, I put my brand-new groceries in the refrigerator. The time I spent with Belmont has somehow energized me. I feel resilient enough to check my email. Could a few kisses and being felt up by a sexy man I met on an impulsive trip to a New England island make me forget the pain of a ten-year relationship gone awry? I didn't think I was that fickle.

I go to the office at the back of the house. The room looks out over the Edgartown Bay. My laptop and notebooks are already sitting on the desk. I must've put them there when I arrived. The sad truth is I can't remember doing it. I turn on the computer and find a significant number of emails from Maya, my former best friend. I hesitate before clicking the last one she sent.

I called your mom and told her what happened. She's worried about you. She wants you to call her. Let's talk, Daisy. It's not what you think.

Mom? Worried? Right. I roll my eyes and read the message she sent three hours before that one.

Adrian wants to explain himself. Will you listen?

Two hours before that.

I don't want to throw fifteen years of friendship down the drain. Adrian and I love each other, but I'll tell him to go fuck himself if that's what you want.

I sniff cynically. The heck she will. I decide to write her back so that she'll stop emailing me.

Maya, I'm on assignment for a month. I'll call you when I return. We'll talk then.

I push send and then search for all the emails she's ever sent—opened and unopened—and delete them. I do the same for all of my replies to her. I want her gone for good.

There are four messages from Adrian. After contemplating opening the last one he sent, I brave forward and click on it.

I told Maya to delete all the pictures and status updates off Facebook. Let's talk. Call me because I can't reach you. Love, Adrian.

I gasp, disgusted. "'Love, Adrian!'"

Love?

My headache returns with a vengeance.

I shut off the computer and stomp upstairs to take a bath. Hot water and a little steam are the fastest ways to reduce my anger

The tub is an old-fashioned claw foot one. I strip out of my dress and underwear, lift my hair into a high ponytail, and wait for the tub to fill. Suddenly, I'm reliving that kiss. Belmont's lips are so soft. Should a man have such supple lips? I slide my thumb across my lower lip. Everything that happened today could not be real.

When, by chance, I glance at the water, I rush to turn it off. It almost overflowed.

I slowly and carefully enter the bubble bath until I'm submerged up to my neck.

"'Love, Adrian,'" I whisper with my eyes closed. "'Love, Adrian.'"

Could he be that self-centered? Why couldn't he have signed, "I screwed your friend while we were still together because I hate and despise you-Adrian"?

On that note, I sink all the way into the tub and let the water bury me. One. Two. Three. Four. The seconds tick by. You can do it. I encourage myself to refuse to come up for air until I'm free of the anger, embarrassment, and pain.

"No, I can't," I wheeze as I break the surface.

Five hours, after my long bath, I stand in front of the mirror, contemplating whether or not I should go through the trouble of taking the car out of the garage, plugging the address in the GPS, and navigating in the dark. A week-long sleeping and crying binge has made my brown skin chalky. On a good note, my eyes aren't red, and I credit the fresh New England air for that.

I brush on a little mascara and slide on some lip gloss. Too much makeup makes me look like a caricature. I have doe eyes, so it appears as if I have natural eyeliner and the apples of my cheeks naturally develop a red undertone, especially when I'm flustered or embarrassed or attracted or something. I bet a million dollars that tonight Belmont Lord will make me feel all three.

My clothes are still in the suitcase, so I take some time to neatly put them away, except for a stretchy, knee-kissing dress made of white fabric with pink and red silkscreen roses. I shimmy into it, put on a pair of red, flat strappy sandals, and fluff out my thick and wavy hair.

I fish the car keys out of a drawer near the back door in the kitchen and hit the road before I change my mind. I keep the top down on the Mini Cooper even though the night is cool. My stomach turns the closer I get to my destination. The forest on both sides of the road runs deep and dark. There's still a lot of traffic. It's not the 405 or 101 rush-hour type, but for the size of the roads and the lack of city amenities, it's still a little too busy.

Make a right on Winter Road, the navigator says.

I make that right.

Your destination is on the left.

Cars are parked along the edge of the tree line across from another colossal, gray, shingled New England colonial.

The home stretches from one end of the property to the other. There's a lot of house on this large lot, and the smell of the nearby ocean tints the air. I park between two gigantic pickup trucks and step onto the white pebbles that cover the surface of the motor court. A Jeep and another truck roll up the gravelly drive, and seeing them puts pep in my step. Not knowing anyone but the birthday boy is awkward enough without running into strangers at the front door. I've crashed weddings and parties before but only to add flair to my articles. This is a totally different ordeal. I've been thinking about the way he kissed me and squeezed my nipple all day long.

At the top of the wraparound porch, a sign saying, "Get Your Ass In Here" is taped onto the red, wood door, which is cracked open. I take a deep breath and follow instructions.

The faint sounds of instruments mixed with chatter—including laughter and a few overly excited, drunken females' voices—fill the air. My feet want to run me back to the car, but the people who arrived after me are on my heels. There's no turning back.

I hurry through a short corridor with an arched ceiling and into a wide-open living room filled with people. The guests stand in groups, talking and drinking: beer in bottles, liquor in high-balls, cocktails, martinis, and wine. A group of people lounges on a large, comfy mustard-colored sectional, focusing on a card game being played on a short, marble-topped table by four people on beanbag chairs. Plopped in front of the fireplace is the source of the music. A group sits around two guys strumming guitars and one blowing the harmonica. There are about fifty or more attendees in all and most are couples.

Suddenly, I'm being observed in the way that strangers amongst friends are examined. Normally, that doesn't make me uncomfortable. If I'm working on an article, I try to act natural, like I belong. Tonight, my eyes dart neurotically around the room in search of that one familiar face. When they locate him, he's standing behind me, staring at me with a weird grimace.

A few seconds pass and he doesn't advance in my direction. The girl he met at the ferry walks up beside him. She says something to him, but he doesn't respond, nor does his expression change.

I'm wondering if he's lost his mind. He looks as if he's angry to see me. I instinctively turn toward the doorway. Right before I run out of here, he walks toward me. He's still watching me in that intense way.

"Seven minutes to spare," he says when he reaches me, frowning at his wristwatch.

"Seven minutes to spare?" I ask.

"It's seven fifty-three." He scans me from head to toe and toe to head. "You look beautiful—sexy." The same scowl returns.

"Are you sure?" He sure isn't looking at me as if he finds me beautiful.

"Very." He leans toward me and puts his mouth against my hair near my ear. "Too beautiful. And you smell good."

We stare into each other's eyes. I should not be feeling whatever this is. I'm still pissed off at Adrian and Maya! I'm still a woman scorned, not a woman falling fast for a strange man on a work trip.

"Would you like a drink?" he asks without breaking eye contact.

"Sure," I squeak.

"What will you have—besides me?" He smirks, entertained by his own joke.

"What are you serving?" I catch myself. I can't believe how flirtatious that sounded.

"Whatever the hell you want."

This time, I put on a less-seductive voice. "Do you have a burgundy?"

"Red or white?"

"Red."

To my surprise, he gives me a quick peck on the lips before saying, "I'll be back."

I watch his tall, elegant frame saunter past the full bar and through a short hall which I suspect leads to the kitchen. It seems as though the entire room saw what just happened. Suddenly I'm being observed more curiously. I stare down at my feet in my strappy sandals, counting the seconds until Belmont returns.

I'm not sure how long it's been since Belmont trotted off to pour me a drink, but I'm getting restless. I scan the room nervously. I'm still being watched. A door is cracked open behind my left shoulder. I play a game with myself. If wherever that door leads takes me to the front of the house, then I'll leave and tell Belmont I didn't feel well if he appears on my doorstep tomorrow.

And so, I step through the door and onto another wide porch. I'm surrounded by comfy patio furniture. There are two longue chaises, one on each side of the door, and a bulky

31

chair has been placed on each side of them. From where I stand, I can see a dark ocean rolling onto the shore and the shadow of a rocky island in the distance. I'm compelled to sit on the foot of the chaise and let my eyes consume the wonderful beyond.

It's nice and quiet in the night air. Colorful potted flowers hang from the decorative spandrels, lending to the sanctity of the moment. Finally, I'm not so uptight. This is what beautiful, exotic destinations were made for–to provide moments of transcendence. Adrian, Maya, and the absent Belmont Lord, who owns the view I'm enjoying, are far from my mind.

Then I hear music. It's coming from the lawn below. I stretch my neck to see a man walking in my direction, strumming a guitar. I search to my left, then to my right to plot an escape. Unfortunately, there isn't one. Both sides of the porch are enclosed. I would have to leap over the banister and drop about five feet in order to get out of here unseen—but probably not unscathed.

Instead, I watch him approach. He has shoulder-length hair and is wearing dark Bermuda shorts but no shirt. The ripped muscles in his chest and calves are simply gorgeous. He's climbing the steps. There are tattoos on his lower legs, shoulders, and one of a misty sun on his chest. His dull brown facial hair is at odds with his bright blue, curious eyes that watch me carefully. I'm immobilized.

He's playing a light, romantic melody, perfect for this kind of night. I expect him to walk right past me and into the house to join his friends in front of the fireplace. However, he gets comfortable on the fluffy patio chair next to me.

He's watching me as he plays his song. Can this get any more awkward? Thank God he finally stops picking the strings to ask, "You're her?"

"I'm her?" I'm confused.

"You're the girl from the docks. Belmont's been bragging about you." His eyes gleam appreciatively. "But he's not your type. I am."

"Sorry?" I say again, wondering if he seriously just said that.

"Forget it," he mutters. "Daisy, right?"

"Um-hum," I reply suspiciously.

"So, Daisy, what brings you to Shitty Island?"

"Shitty Island?"

His eyes dance as he stares at my face. I can tell that he's enjoying the effect he's having on me. "That's my name for it. But really, why are you here? Vacation? Newbie?"

"Work," I quickly answer.

"It's a bad time to find a job on the island, but I can hire you. I'm in the market for a personal assistant…" He smirks naughtily.

"I'm a travel writer," I quickly explain.

"And you're writing a story about Shitty Island in the autumn? Should've come in the summer. At least your story could've been a little interesting."

I shrug, slightly put off by his forwardness. "I don't know. Look at that view. That's what traveling is all about."

His eyes follow mine.

"Plus," I continue, "I have golden fingers. I can make a slap of earth in the middle of nowhere sound like paradise." I'm definitely tooting my own horn.

"Then I should take you to Noman's Land."

"Oh," I say with a roll of the eyes, "you're joking."

He chuckles condescendingly. "You're really cute. But there's really a spot near the island called Noman's Land."

"Is that so?" I'm intrigued enough to forget how patronizing he sounds.

"That is so," he assures me.

"No man's land? Like no man lives there?"

"Noman's Land. One word: Noman's."

"Noman's?" I repeat.

"Noman's," he confirms.

We fall silent. I can't believe it, but we're grinning at each other. There's something familiar about the contours of his face and the shape of his eyes.

"Are you related to Belmont?" I blurt out.

One side of his mouth lifts into a severe smirk. "He's my brother."

"I see the resemblance."

"So you came all the way to Shitty Island by yourself?" he asks, quickly changing the subject. He doesn't look happy about what I just said.

"Why do you call it that? This place is beautiful."

"It's shitty for me."

"Then why don't you leave? You look like an adult to me."

He grins for a long time before saying, "Where the hell will I go?"

"Anywhere you want."

Once again, we're staring quietly into each other's eyes. I kind of like the tricky conversation we're having. Belmont's brother is certainly an interesting specimen. Just for a moment,

I wonder if I could replace him with Belmont, which is sort of insane since, other than a few kisses, Belmont and I aren't romantically involved.

"No boyfriend?" he asks out of the blue.

"Not anymore." I look at the active ocean.

"Did you just break up?"

"Yeah," I say with a tired sigh as those old feelings stir inside of me again.

"What happened? Were you too awesome for him?"

"Ha!" I scoff. "Would that be the reason your boyfriend dumps you—but doesn't tell you that you've been dumped—and then ends up engaged to your best friend?" I lift a finger pointedly. "Ex-best friend."

"Hell yeah!" he exclaims, grinning from ear to ear. I see he's joking. Making light of the Jerry Springer-ish ordeal I'm in is welcomed. "Hey, you want to go down to the beach?"

I glance over my shoulder, wondering what in the world happened to Belmont. "Well, Belmont was supposed to bring me a drink, but I think he got lost." I frown at the door, waiting for him to open it at any second.

"I've got us covered," he says. He feels under his chair and pulls out one and then two wine bottles filled with reddish-brown liquid. "Follow me." He leaps to his feet.

I recoil. "What's that?"

"My special brew."

"Brew of what?"

"Don't worry. You'll like it. I promise."

Before I can stall in hopes that the brother I'm more interested in will open the door behind me with a glass of burgundy in hand, the other brother is off. In a fraction of a second, I decide to follow. We walk beside each other across a lawn, past a guesthouse that's been fashioned out of a barn, and down worn cement steps leading to the beach. Four sets of Adirondack chairs are plopped in the sand, facing the great blue sea. A little farther down, I see a stack of wood waiting to be set ablaze for the big bonfire.

As I walk, I kick up grains of sand, and many of them are trapped under my feet and between my toes.

"Ah ha," Belmont's brother says. I rip my eyes from the ocean to see that he's produced two wine glasses from a portable cooler that was already there.

I study how the moonlight presses down on the surface of the water as he pours the liquid in the bottle into the glasses. I've always found the Atlantic Ocean more ominous than the Pacific. It's as if the great beyond is pacing feverishly along the coast, steaming mad that dry land dares to exist. It's threatening but exquisite.

"Here you go," he says as he hands me the glass.

I take it. The concoction has a rigid but fruity scent.

"It's nice out there," he says, gazing ahead as he guzzles whatever's in the glass.

"It is." I take a sip. I'm surprised by the taste. "Mm, this is good."

He lifts his eyebrows. "Told you."

Belmont's brother is cute. He's just as sexy as Belmont but in a different way—in an earthy way. He reminds me of the boys surfing the south California beaches, going down toward San Diego County—the ones who look as if they'll only take a bath if they're riding a surfboard.

"By the way, what's your name?"

He snickers. "I was wondering when you were going to ask. It's Charlie."

"Belmont and Charlie," I muse.

"Formally Charles. Our parents had high hopes, and all they got was us."

"Are you blue-blooded?" I ask, taking a healthier swig of my drink.

"Royal blue."

I gag, nearly choking. "Are you royalty?" I cough.

He laughs and slaps me on the back. "All good?"

I clear the last bit of liquid out of my windpipe. "Yeah. You can move your hand now." He's enjoying rubbing on my back a little too much.

He removes his hand. "The answer to your question is no. Ever heard of Lord's Steel?"

I shake my head. "No."

"That's because it's not around anymore. We sold it, split the cash..." He stops as though he's choosing to leave something out.

"How does that relate to the 'high hopes'?" I ask.

His expression grows dim. "Our parents are dead." He steps toward the Adirondacks. "Let's sit." Charlie slumps into one of the wood chairs, and I trot across the sand like a Clydesdale to take the one beside him. He's still sullen, and instead of drinking out of the glass, he guzzles from the bottle. The alcohol is already working on my head, making me a little dizzy.

It's clearly time to change the subject. I close my eyes to sigh. "I didn't understand why your brother was interested in me. I'm not his type." Was being the operative word. Maybe he used me to make the blonde jealous. He looks like the type that would take such drastic measures.

Charlie utters a tsk. "Why the hell are you interested in him?" He extends the bottle to top off my glass.

"How do you know I'm interested?" I ask as he pours. My words are dragging.

"You're all interested. Girls like him. He's got magic," he mumbles sarcastically. "You're sitting here, watching the ocean. Do you like the way it sounds?"

"Love it," I say before taking another swallow.

"You respect it, don't you?" he asks in a serious tone.

"Very much."

"You're too deep for him. He's a rigid asshole, and you'll get bored."

"Or he'll get bored."

"Nah, he won't." Charlie sounds sure about that.

"Oh yes, he will. And you would too. Didn't I tell you…" Jeez, I already forgot what I was going to say. I'm officially intoxicated.

"Didn't you tell me what?"

Shucks. My head is spinning. "Didn't I tell you that my boyfriend left me for my best friend? She's obviously the desirable one." I close my eyes and inhale the fresh, crisp beach air. Clips of Maya run through my head. "She's always there, you know? Smiling and extra nice while I shrink into the background. A shrinking violet, that's what I am…"

He snorts cynically and holds out the bottle to pour me another. "Oh, she's one of those kinds of girls."

"Yeah, likable. Desirable." I should pass on the refill, but I don't.

"More like competitive. Easy." He fills my glass to the rim.

"She's not easy," I scold, which is surprising. Am I seriously defending her after what she's done to me?

"You're smart, Daisy. I can tell. Deep down, you know what I'm talking about. I dine on chicks like her."

We fall silent as I think. Maya does like to be the center of attention, and I allow it. I'm certainly not comfortable standing behind her, looking stupid as my mind processes everything that's going on. She's quicker than I am. Like the time we were having lunch at the Patio Galley Café off Venice Beach. Two firefighters sat at the table next to ours and appraised us admiringly. I've been all over the world, and the firefighters in Los Angeles are the only ones who live up to the cliché. If I were sitting there alone, I would've never said one word to them. I would've opened my notebook and worked on an article. Plus, I had a boyfriend. But not Maya—she always flirts.

She'd started a conversation with them that lasted an entire hour. First, she commented on how big their feet were in their work boots. Every time one of them tried to include me in the discussion about what parts of the city they were called out to the most, Maya would subtly remind them that I had a boyfriend.

"Oh, her boyfriend lives in that area."

"Oh, her boyfriend worked at the studio when it caught fire."

"Oh, Daisy's boyfriend said that too."

What caught me off guard was that one of the firemen said, "Oh, is that your name? Daisy? Like the flower?" He seemed upset that Maya monopolized the entire conversation.

He and I smiled at each other, but then Maya found a way to focus his attention back on her. She dropped her fork near his big foot and leaned across the aisle to get it. She made sure he got an eyeful of her perfect, perky 34D implants—which she'd fashioned after my 34C real ones. I turned to look dejectedly over the boardwalk.

Maya and the firefighter ended up exchanging phone numbers. They went on a few dates before, according to her, she got bored and decided to cut things off with him.

Maybe Charlie's right. Maybe she wasn't interested in that firefighter until we smiled at each other.

Struck by enlightenment, I look at Charlie. He's already staring at me. I think we're caught in a moment. Then I hear a familiar voice say, "There you are!"

Charlie and I quickly look behind us. It's Belmont, and he has a glass of wine.

"The burgundy you requested," he says, staring daggers at his brother.

"That's okay," I say and lift the glass in my hand. "I already have a drink. Charlie's special brew."

Charlie is facing the ocean. I'm the only one smiling. Of course, I should be angry with Belmont, but I'm not. After my talk with Charlie, the ocean, and the spirits, I feel as though I can finish out my two weeks, write a spectacular article, and move on with my life. Yet the moment is awkward. I'm not sure who Belmont is angry with: Charlie or me.

"When I came back to find you, you were gone," Belmont says in an accusatory tone.

Twisting in the chair to look at him feels awkward, so I rise to my feet. "I…" Then my weakened knees give out. I fall back down in the chair and drop my glass, spilling the red liquid.

Belmont is right there to collect me, lifting me out of the chair with one arm and holding me against him. Jeez. My head feels as if ducks are revolving around it. The side of my face is pressed against his hard, warm chest.

I listen to his heartbeat as he growls, "What the hell are you doing, Chuck?"

Before Charlie can respond, Belmont whisks me up and walks me carefully up the stairs.

"I can call a cab," I burble.

"You're not calling a cab, Daisy," he grumbles. "You can sleep it off in one of the guest rooms."

"No, I can call a cab," I insist.

"There'll be no cab calling," he says as if that's final. Belmont sets the glass of burgundy down on the stoop of the guesthouse and walks me to an unlit part of the main house. He fishes keys out of his pocket and unlocks the back door. Since I'm dizzy and groggy, I close my eyes as he leads me up another flight of curving stairs. I walk blindly until I make contact with a fluffy duvet on top of a soft bed.

One by one, Belmont removes my sandy sandals. Then there's nothing: not a sound, no more touching. I struggle to lift my heavy eyelids, and I see my caretaker standing at the side of the bed, gazing at me.

"I didn't mean to drink too much. I only had a glass and a half," I manage to say. "Maybe two."

"I'm not blaming you. I blame Chuck. I'm not going to leave you by yourself in this condition."

"I'll be fine." He watches me intensely as I curl up. "I'll sleep it off in two hours. You can go back to the party." I mumble something about the bonfire I already regret missing.

The next thing I know, the bed dips as his body settles beside me. Plop—one of Belmont's shoes hits the floor and then the other.

"It's not you that I'm worried about." He stretches out. Our faces are close. "Daisy?"

"Yes?" I croak, unable to open my eyes. I'm not so out of it that I can't hear the yearning in his voice.

"Will you let me hold you?"

I gulp and nod against the most comfortable pillow I've ever laid my head on.

Belmont reaches over to rotate my body, and now he's spooning me. His ready bulge is pressed against the crease of my butt. My heart starts thumping, my nipples stiffen, and my body craves more of him. However, I have no plans to go all the way. After all, I only met him today and in the fragile state that I'm in, there's no way of trusting my own emotions or desires. Maybe I'm simply vulnerable. Maybe I'm on the rebound.

But his body does feel like heaven against mine.

"Daisy?" His voice warms my ear.

"Humph?" I hum comfortably.

"What's my type if you're not my type?"

"Huh?" I'm wide awake now. "You heard that?"

"Every word. So what's my type?"

I shrug.

"Stay still," he warns and then grinds his package against my tender bottom. "Please," he pleads vulnerably. His fingers strum my belly and work their way up to my breasts.

I try not to moan. I want him to stop and to keep going just the same. I want to throw common sense and caution to the wind and let him have my body. I clasp his hand to stop him. "Please," I say in the same tone he just used.

He chuckles, and it sounds so sexy. "All right, but you haven't answered my question."

"What do I think your type is?" I ask.

"Yes."

"More Barbie-ish."

"You mean blonde?"

"Barbie comes in all colors. But they all have the same hair, makeup, stilettos, and plastic. There's nothing wrong with it. It's just far from who I am."

"Do you really believe I'm that shallow?"

"I don't know. You just have a look about you." I yawn. "When I saw you, I said, 'Not his type, not my type.'"

"When did you first see me?"

"On the pier."

"Did you see me staring at you?"

"No," I whisper.

"I wanted you then. But you're wrong about me, Daisy."

"I am?" I mutter.

"You are."

A long moment of silence lingers. I'm halfway asleep. I've never felt this comfortable in a man's arms. I feel like if I sleep, then he'll slay any dragon and conquer any army that seeks to destroy me in my dreams.

"Daisy," I hear him ask faintly.

"Humph…"

"Are you asleep?"

"Humph…"

I feel his package grind against me a few times. His lips kiss the back of my neck. Then he takes my shoulder and guides me around to face him. Our lips and tongues lock. Our kiss is deep and passionate. My head is spinning for so many different reasons, but my escalating dopamine levels caused by arousal is the main one.

"That's all I'll take from you for now," he whispers as he sucks on my neck one last time. Belmont gently helps me face away from him, and he wraps his arms around me. He squeezes me tightly. Once again, I feel safe.

He says something in my ear but I'm already dreaming about floating on the raging Atlantic Ocean. I'm naked, and the sun is directly above me. I have a feeling that Charlie is sitting in the Adirondack chair observing me. Suddenly, Belmont is lying on top of me, and together we are being pulled into the deep, clear water. I'm waiting to drown. I'm waiting to hit bottom. But we're just staring into each other's eyes, falling into forever.

I open my eyes.

It's morning.

I'm in bed alone, in a strange room, slowly recalling the events of the night that led me here.

CHAPTER 4

There's A First Time For Everything

"Sleep well?"

Startled, I sit up. Belmont is standing in front of one of the large panel windows that are standard for Colonials this size. Tamed light filters in from outside. I have to blink him into focus.

He certainly looks nice. Belmont is wearing a pair of dark-blue jeans and a well-fitting, pale gray, lightweight sweater. His look is effortless—down to his barely there and immaculately trimmed facial hair. Basically, his appearance is crisp and clean while I look and feel like a mess.

"What?" My arms spastically fly up to scrunch down my wild hair. I have mounds of it. I've been asked a million times if I wear a wig, but nope, it's my own personal cumulus cloud.

Then it all comes back—drinking his brother's—Chuck or Charlie—special brew. Their parents are dead, and they're blue-blooded. But the most momentous recollection is that Belmont said he wants me and has "wanted me" from the first time he saw me.

I lift the thick blanket to get a look at myself. I'm relieved to see I'm still fully clothed and in last night's dress. A faint taste of the special brew is still on my tongue.

"I have to brush my teeth," I say as I kick off the covers. "I have to go." My only goal is to escape to where no one can see me like this. Not even Adrian ever saw me look this disheveled.

"No way." Belmont takes two large steps and stops in front of me. "I made breakfast."

"But I have to brush my teeth, wash my face. I look terrible."

He cracks a tiny smile. "I didn't think you cared about all of that. Only a 'Barbie' would be that self-conscious."

"Well I like to have fresh breath and a clean face and tamer hair," I grumble.

"I like your hair like that. It's sexy."

I grunt, pondering that. "I also prefer it this way, but Adrian didn't," I reveal.

"This Adrian guy is starting to sound more and more like a major asshole."

"No," I sigh. "He's not that. He's just..." I can't put him into rational words. "I just always felt like I had to be someone other than me with him. That's probably why I loved him more when we had distance between us."

"Come here," Belmont says as he holds his arms out for me.

I latch on to his hands, and he lifts me into his arms. Against my better judgment, we kiss. A moan escapes him as he ends with a tiny bite on my top, then bottom lip.

"You taste intoxicating." We chuckle. "But there's a fresh toothbrush and towels for you in the bathroom."

"Which way?" My head is spinning.

He points to the right. "That way." He's grinning, completely aware of his effect on me. Belmont still has his arms around my waist.

Even though we're gazing into each other's eyes, I haven't committed to the embrace the way he has. My arms hang by my side. This cannot be happening. There's no way I'm falling for him. Is he still a stranger? I feel as if we've known each other our entire lives. However, I do have a question to ask.

"By the way, who's the blonde? The one you met at the docks? She was at the party last night, and she didn't look happy to see me."

He forces a hard breath out his nose. I sense I hit a nerve. I shake my head and pull out of his arms. "I'm leaving." Before I can spin around and stomp off, I'm securely in his arms.

"That was Kara. She's my ex-girlfriend."

"Does she know she's your ex-girlfriend?"

"Of course."

"Then why is she here?"

"Because we're still friends."

"With benefits?" I've learned to keep the questions coming quickly; it gives the answerer less time to consider lying.

"Yes. No. Not after yesterday."

I shake my head. "This is crazy."

He nods. "I know. I didn't expect any of this."

"But you made it happen!" I accuse.

"If you think I do this sort of thing often, I don't. Kara and I are off, and she can't get over it. I told her that last night. That's why it took me so long to get your wine." He sniffs bitterly. "Which was enough time for Chuck to make a move."

"But why is she here? Wouldn't it be easier for her if she weren't?" I can't let it drop. I mean, goodness, she and I could be standing in the same heartbroken shoes!

"She's in a wedding today. Look, on my part, it was nothing. She called me and asked if I could pick her up from the ferry. I said yes. I saw you, and I wasn't the same. But we did have dinner, she came over and put the moves on me, the way I wished you would. I don't know... I thought my fascination with you was unreasonable, so I tried to forget about it. She and I... we did it."

"Had sex?"

"Yes," he whispers, regretfully. "It fucking feels like I cheated on you."

"You didn't cheat on me." Even I have to admit that. "You didn't even know me." No, it's Adrian who cheated on me!

I blow out a forceful sigh. This entire ordeal is strange, to say the least. Sex with the ex-girlfriend one night, then chase me and insist that I attend his party the next day. What if I'm a game? What if he's one of those guys who are turned on by the chase? Will he vanish once he catches me?

He tilts his head curiously. "What is it?"

I make an on-the-spot decision. He's sexy, and I need this little diversion. I don't need another man playing trampoline on my heart. If he wants to play cat and mouse, then I'll let him catch me, screw me, and there, fun had, chase over.

I go in for the kiss, and he responds. I can feel that he's turned on. His heart is racing against mine, and he's quivering.

"Are you sure?" he pants against my parted lips.

This is stupid, but my body craves this fling. It'll be short and sweet, and when we part ways, it will be forever.

"Isn't this what you want?" I sigh as he bites and sucks on the side of my neck.

He stops abruptly. "What does that mean?" He's grimacing.

"You want to have sex with me, right?"

"Yes, but that's not all."

"Belmont…" My tone is patronizing. I pat his chest. "I have an article to write. Thank you for providing a bed last night, but…"

He exhales sharply through his nose and shakes his head. "This is it."

"What's it?"

"This could be the reason your boyfriend left you." I gasp, offended, and try to pull myself out of his grasp, but he holds me tighter. "You're assuming something about me but you haven't let me know what that is. You're not giving me a chance to defend myself. I don't want you to leave. I do want to have sex with you, but I want more too. Do I know what that is? No. I just want to be around you. I knew that when I first saw you, and then when I saw you yesterday—after thinking about you all night long—I couldn't let the chance to get to know you pass."

I have no immediate response. After a moment of studying my expression, he plants a tender kiss on the tip of my nose. He knows how to touch and kiss very well. He's very sensual and affectionate. He knows how to make me putty in his hands. I want to run away with him into whatever fairytale Prince Charming rode his white horse out of.

"I want to do something to you and for you," he says, grinning seductively.

"What?" I squeak past my constricted vocal cords. I swallow.

Slowly, he guides me down on top of the bed. My heart is pounding so hard that I can feel the vibrations in my throat. He takes my dress by the hem and ceremoniously slides it up my thighs.

I'm studying him, wondering what in the world is he going to do. A man has never put his face so close to my private parts. Belmont's teeth and lips work in unison as they kiss and gently nibble their way up the inside of my thighs.

"Shit, you're soft," he whispers sensually.

As soon as his lips land on my crotch, I gasp.

"You're wet…" He's apparently turned on by the moisture.

I'm tingling all over but especially down there. I've never felt that spark of sensations.

"You smell good," he whispers throatily.

"Ah!" I cry and grab the messy bed sheets. He's latched on to what I think is my clitoris. I squirm and jerk.

"Relax, baby," he says and takes my panties by the sides. He pulls them down my legs, kissing as he goes.

"What are you doing?" I lift myself on my elbows to watch him wide-eyed.

"You really don't know what I'm going to do?" He looks up from between my legs, amused. I shake my head. "No one's ever gone down on you before, Daisy?"

I shake my head. "No."

A huge smile appears on his lips. "Oh shit, a virgin."

"I'm not a virgin." I sound defensive, although being a virgin wouldn't be so bad.

"Have you ever had an orgasm?"

"Yeah…" I sound uncertain because if an orgasm feels anything like what he just did to me, then maybe I haven't.

"Well we're about to find out, aren't we?" He kisses the insides of my thighs again, and then his hot, wet tongue returns to that spot.

I inhale as if I've been socked in the stomach and bite down on my bottom lip. What in the world is he doing to me? I clutch the bed spread, but the material seems too weak to brace myself on. Belmont offers no reprieve. On the contrary, he's lifted my crotch closer to his face and has clamped his arms around my rear end. I can't even move an inch. However, his grip doesn't stop me from squirming and thrashing my upper body against the mattress.

"Oh no!" I cry. I lift my head to see how he's doing that, and our eyes meet. But not for long. My lower half trembles. The most intense feeling ever seizes me. I'm overcome by a sensation akin to the signal of a ready teakettle. My entire vagina is whistling and pulsing. I scream, moan, and whimper. I experience some sort of white out when the full force of it hits. I think I have Belmont by the shoulders. My fingernails dig into his skin. When whatever that was passes, I am able to release the tension in my body and breathe again, although I'm panting.

"That"—his tongue rounds my clit again, and I grab a handful of blanket—"was an orgasm," he whispers.

"Then, no," I say breathlessly. "I've never had one of those."

"How about two?"

I'm both exhilarated and alarmed. I guess it shows on my face because he shows me that wicked smile before starting all over again.

This time, the fingers of one of his strong hands stroke my waist and stomach indulgently. He slides two fingers, I think, inside of me. Not too deep. They're slipping against the inside of my pubic bone.

I cry out as soon as sparks of that teakettle sensation strike me. I twist and turn and arch my back. The more I move, the more he groans. His fingers find what they're looking for and draw circles around that sensitive spot.

I'm caught in euphoria.

It's coming…

Coming…

I'm coming!

I'm screaming, maybe crying until he's on top of me.

"Taste yourself, baby," he whispers as his teeth and lips gather my bottom lip into his mouth. "Shit, you're sweet."

We are kissing deeper than ever. His tongue might touch the back of my throat, and his penis is as hard as a boulder. He's stabbing me with it. He's rubbing it up and down my shifting pubic bone, stimulating me.

Suddenly he unlatches his belt, unbuttons and unzips his pants, and eagerly plugs me with his full-on erection. Oh goodness gracious, we're having sex!

His strokes are slow, indulgent.

"You're so tight," he mutters, "so wet."

I feel the material of his jeans and sweater against me. His mouth and tongue haven't pulled away from mine since he said I'm wet. He's aroused me beyond a level I've ever reached. Even if this is our only time together, if I was right and he chased me to make this moment happen, then I have no regrets. Barely thirty-five years old, ten of those years as Adrian's girlfriend, and I finally know what a real orgasm feels like.

Belmont freezes. His penis is pushed deep inside of me. He stops kissing me to look into my eyes. He's wearing a strained expression.

"What is it?" I ask.

"I don't want to come yet. But..."

He increases the speed of his strokes. He's moving so fast that my insides are tickled, and I'm on the verge of experiencing my third orgasm ever. I'm moaning and grab handfuls of his damp sweater. He grunts and trembles and then collapses on top of me before I can fully finish.

One side of Belmont's head is pressed against my cheek. We're both breathing heavily. The seconds tick by, and he still hasn't budged. I'm trying to think of what to say next.

"So where do we start?" he asks before I can form my own words.

"I'm not sure what you're talking about."

"With the article we have to write for you."

I snicker and his lips find mine.

"There's nothing better than kissing your mouth"—he pauses thoughtfully—"other than eating you out and this." He pushes his blossoming hard-on inside of me.

I have no response to what he just said. He seems to be getting a kick out of having sex with me. I don't know if Adrian ever derived that much pleasure from my body. He had two modes: missionary and doggy-style. He was okay at it. He liked to pinch my nipples and suck on them until they're sore. He always came pretty fast, which was why we usually had sex multiple times in one session. There was lots of passion between us—lots of caressing and hugging. I'm sure he desired me all the way up until the end.

"I'll never stop if we stay like this," Belmont finally proclaims. He carefully pulls himself out of me and uses the sheet to catch his spill off.

"We didn't use a condom," I whisper, horrified.

"Don't worry. I always use condoms."

I watch him wipe his thick penis with the comforter. "Yeah, right," I say doubtfully.

He tilts his head. "You don't believe me?"

"No, I don't," I reply without hesitation.

"It's true."

"Did you use a condom the other night with Kara?"

"I did, but I couldn't stay up. I didn't even come." He's already pulled up his pants, and he's zipping them.

"We still were very negligent," I say as I slide off the bed.

"You and I are together, so it isn't."

I laugh. "You're insane," I joke, thinking he couldn't really mean that.

"We are. No condom means girlfriend."

I stop looking for my panties to study him. Although his eyes have a bouncy look, he's certainly serious.

"This is how it happens when we're meant to be, Daisy," he says. He's studying me, still grinning. He's trying to read my reaction.

I certainly have the same irrational emotions that he has. I mean—could it happen like this? Is this how true love and fifty-year anniversaries began? Do they start with two people who know absolutely nothing about each other, other than knowing deep down they'll never be apart? That's how I feel. I finally locate my panties. "If you say so."

"Then it's settled. I'll let Charlie know so he can stop hitting on you. If he does it again, I'll break his neck." He winks at me just to clue me in that he's joking. He slides his leather belt through the buckle and tugs. "Don't worry, babe, I'm not violent. He won't listen to me anyway. He's going to keep trying until he has you in his bed."

"Charlie's never going to have me in his bed," I say, very sure of that.

Belmont takes me by the arm and I smash into his strong chest. "That's what I wanted to hear."

We kiss. Nothing's changed since he declared us a couple. His lips and tongue are still greedy and eager to meet mine.

"Did I mention that your skin is soft?" he whispers between kisses.

"Yes, you did," I manage to say.

"How about we stay in bed for the rest of the day?"

That's when my stomach growls long and hard. It's so embarrassing that I hide my face against his chest.

He laughs and takes my chin, lifting my face. "I take that back. How about we eat first, and then crawl into bed for the rest of the day?"

I chuckle, no longer mortified. "How about we eat and then get to work on my article? Plus I have to email the editor. I think adding this destination to my taxi series—"

Suddenly his warm tongue is wrapped around mine. When he's done, he says, "You're a workaholic. And every time you have an episode, I'm going to punish you."

My eyebrows pull together. I'm perplexed. "Punish me how?"

Belmont takes my shoulders and guides me back to the edge of the bed to sit. He guides my back down onto the mattress and lifts my legs over his shoulders.

I gasp in anticipation of what he might do next. Oh my, is he going to do it again–pleasure me?

His mouth consumes one swollen lip of my vagina and then the other. I cry out as soon as his wet tongue connects with my "ON" button and he commences to punish me for thinking about work. I hear myself breathing heavily while realizing he's going to be punishing me a lot because I'm always thinking about work.

Belmont gave me three more orgasms before my stomach warned him again that I need food. So he reluctantly left me alone to freshen up.

I'm slowly raking the brush across my teeth, wondering if I have a new boyfriend or not. I feel as if the last nine days never happened. My heart doesn't ache anymore. Maya and Adrian aren't distant memories, but when I think of them, my mind doesn't conjure the image of the two of them screwing like soft-porn stars.

I splash my face with warm water and use a fluffy red towel to dry it. The linens, the bedspread, and towels are all five-star quality. One thing's for sure: Belmont has impeccable taste, right down to his Cavalli sneakers. Believe me, I noticed.

As soon as I turn off the faucet, I hear a faint knock on the bedroom door. I give myself a final once-over. I'm glad Belmont likes my hair like this. Whenever I know I'm going to be trapped inside for a week, drinking coffee and writing, the first thing I do is wash the straight right out of my hair. I get the makeup off my face and put on a long baseball T-shirt and leg-warmers.

There's the knocking again.

"I'm ready!" I say as I trot over to the door, thinking it's Belmont. When I open it, there's Charlie, looking madder than a raging bull. "Hi," I say apprehensively.

"Here's your purse." He shoves the bag at me.

I'm slow to take it, but he doesn't let go. His eyes roam past me to study the messy linens on the bed.

"Did he make you climb the walls, see stars?" he asks in a stinging tone.

My mouth falls open. I'm speechless. He's made me feel so cheap.

"He's good at it, isn't he?" he continues with a cruel expression.

I still don't know what to say.

"Ask him why he's so damn good at fucking you."

On that note, Charlie stomps off down the hallway, still shirtless and wearing the Bermuda shorts from last night.

CHAPTER 5

The Self-Appointed Tour Guide

I'm still vexed by what Charlie said. I walk down the hallway barefooted, carrying my shoes in one hand. The premium hardwood floors are so glossy it should be a crime to trample on them in shoes.

Belmont has taped signs on the walls that say, "Kitchen This Way" with an arrow pointing me in the direction I should go. It's certainly a bit overstated to go through all that trouble, and Charlie has me doubting his brother's authenticity. If that was his goal, then it worked. Why would Charlie know that Belmont's good in bed? It's simply weird. I'm sure he is insinuating that Belmont has had tons of girlfriends, which I've already guessed. I mean, look at him. He's suave. If his "tactics" worked on me, then they'll be as easy as biting into cotton candy if used on the average girl. Normally, I'm not easy to pick up.

When I make it to the kitchen, I see Charlie sitting at the large island separating the fabulous gourmet kitchen from a plush lounge area. The lounge is adorned with a purple velvet three-piece sectional facing a contemporary fireplace that's cut into a glass wall. The beach is the backdrop. It's a magnificent sight

Belmont stops reading the paper to regard me. I'm not sure if that look means he approves of what he sees or not. I'm suddenly aware of the fact that I care, which is not good. He leaps off the stool and rushes over to plant a minty kiss on my lips. "You're sexy," he whispers in my ear. "Stay in with me today."

"Shit, Jack, I'm trying to eat," Charlie grumbles, scowling into his waffles.

"Who's Jack?" I ask, suddenly confused.

"My middle name is Jaxson," Belmont mumbles, glaring at Charlie, who's grinning like he's holding back a secret.

"Like Action Jackson?" I ask, chuckling at my attempt at a joke.

Charlie snorts because he finds it funny.

Belmont just smiles lazily. "Almost. J-a-x-s-o-n."

"Oh, nice." I take a seat at the island in front of a waffle loaded with fresh plump blueberries and sliced strawberries. "Is this for me?"

I gaze at Belmont. He says that I'm sexy, but that road runs both ways. His bright eyes look as if they could perform magic, and the way his top lip curls up toward the tip of his nose gives him a bow-tie smile. I've never seen a man blessed with that feature before, and I've traveled all over the planet. His face is unique.

"All yours." He's flirting with me with those mesmer-izing eyes.

Breakfast looks tasty, and I'm so hungry I dig right in. Usually I'm busy doing something while eating: polishing an article, planning my next pitch, research, reading my colleagues' work etc. Suddenly I feel like I have idle hands. "Do you have a newspaper? The New York Times possibly?" I ask Belmont. I realize that I'm reaching.

He laughs out loud and holds up a finger. He trots from around the breakfast bar and out of sight.

"I thought I'd take us out to Noman's Land today," Charlie says when we're alone.

I frown at him, wondering if he's serious. Just in case Belmont's near, I whisper, "I can't go with you."

"You can do what you want. It's not too late to choose me. We'll take the Columbus."

"What's the Columbus?" I ask, even though in my heart, I've already rejected his offer.

"My speedboat." He's simpering, watching me with starry, hopeful eyes.

"Why do you like me? Is it because Belmont does?" I'm discerning his affections may be the result of sibling rivalry.

Belmont's heavy footsteps approach. Charlie leans in close to whisper, "Because I saw you first." Charlie and I are still looking at each other when Belmont drops a newspaper on the tabletop between us. "Chuck? What are you doing?"

"Asking her if she wants to take a ride with me." Charlie hasn't backed off yet.

"She doesn't," Belmont hisses.

"Are you sure, Jack? We were vibing last night before you showed up. Isn't that right, Daisy?"

My lips part in awe, and Belmont takes my chin to plant a kiss on my mouth with Charlie still only inches away from my face. That one kiss sends me floating as soon as our lips touch.

"She's not going with you, Chuck," Belmont says.

Charlie sits up straight and hops off the stool. "I know. And it's too bad." He flirts with me with his eyes before he heads out, leaving his breakfast half eaten.

"What's up with you two?" I'm forced to ask after Charlie strolls out of sight.

Belmont glares at me accusingly. "If you like him, then…"

I'm waiting for him to finish whatever he was about to say, but he doesn't. "Listen, I like Charlie because he's nice to me—even if he isn't so nice to you—but that's all." I can't be rational and divulge the truth to Belmont at the same time, which is, I can never be into anyone else but him at this juncture.

After a long moment of silence, he nods, accepting my explanation. "I'll make us coffee then. I'll make it strong. I don't want you falling asleep on me when we go back upstairs." He shows me his naughty-boy smirk.

"Yeah… I was thinking about later." I keep my eyes glued to my plate. If I look at him, I might lose my willpower. "I have to do some work today."

What we did upstairs was an epic mistake. I've never had sex with anyone I didn't love, and I couldn't be in love with Belmont so fast. I certainly like him a lot—an awful, awful lot. He's charming, sexy, and seems to adore me for some strange reason. He knows nothing about me really, and vice versa. Maybe he's a psycho. They always charm women in the beginning. He can't be looking to empty my bank account because he's far richer than I am. Our entire encounter is weird. It almost feels like a set-up, a practical joke.

I hop off the stool, determined to go upstairs, retrieve my purse, and head out. "I can see you later tonight though. Maybe you can take me to dinner or something?" I beam at him.

Oh shoot, here he comes. Before I'm able to step back to avoid his embrace, he takes me in his arms.

"Hey…" He lowers his face to look me in the eyes, and my eyes can't avoid his. "If you don't want to stay in bed, that's fine. I got greedy. You want to call a cab to take you around the island? I'll pay for it."

"Why are you coming on so strong?" I ask. "I don't understand."

"Because you're the one, Daisy," he says bluntly. "I know it even if you don't."

"I've seen scenarios like this on TV. Are you a rich guy looking to lure a wife, put a life insurance policy on me, and…?" I use two fingers to slice the air in front of my neck.

Belmont's hazel eyes brighten as he laughs out loud, but I don't laugh with him. I'm dead serious—no pun intended.

"No," he answers as if he's talking to a crazy person. "And if I had those plans, do you think I would tell you?"

My eyes expand with horror. "Wrong answer."

He squeezes me tighter. By the feel of things, he's ready to have sex again. "I'm going to kiss you now," he whispers hoarsely.

My mouth is caught open, giving his tongue space to slip right in there. My lips feel softer lodged between his, and then we taste each other with gentle, warm tongues. He's expertly leading the dance of this kiss. The longer we do this, the more we can't stop. I whimper and sigh. I feel as if I'm floating on air.

Maybe Belmont's right. We are meant to be. We certainly have intense sexual chemistry. Or, as Charlie suggested, maybe he's just good at this.

"Hey," I breathe as I force my lips to part from his.

"What? Do you want to stay in? We can do this and only this. I can make out with you all day and all night long."

My head is spinning. I want to take him up on his offer, but instead I keep my focus. "No, that's not it. It's just that Charlie asked me to ask you why you're so good at 'f'ing' me?"

"What's 'f'ing'?" He's amused by my word choice.

"You know…" I imply, lifting my eyebrows.

"No, I don't." He's feigning ignorance. "Do you mean this?" He grabs my rear end and shoves me into his healthy lump.

"Yes," I sigh. My eyes are closed. He hasn't stopped rubbing me against him. He's making me feel something.

"Because I know a woman's body better than my own. See…" He shifts me against his bulge once and then twice until he shoves me harder, holding me steady. He doesn't ease the tension. My eyes are closed as the tingling sensation builds. I can feel him studying my expression.

It's coming…

I'm close…

I'm so damn close…

Then suddenly I explode. I wrap my arms around him, moaning into his neck, which smells so good. Belmont presses his mouth to mine. He greedily lifts the hem of my dress, spreads my legs, and shoves two fingers inside of me.

"Shit," he mutters as he bites and sucks on my neck. He takes me by the hips and smashes me against his bulge again. I hold tight to him as he shifts me up and down his swollen crotch until he lets out a series of grunts.

When he's done quivering, he goes completely still, stalling my next climax. "I'm sorry, Daisy." His warm breath tickles my ear canal. "That one was for me."

More than likely, I'm influenced by the one and a half orgasms in the kitchen, but I agree to let Belmont call a cab and accompany me on my island expedition. I tell him he's not allowed to pay or interfere in any way.

After Belmont changed his soiled pants and underwear and talked me into venturing out without panties—since he made mine all wet—we walk up the winding dirt path from his house cut between the forest on our way to State Road. Along the way, he keeps tugging at my skirt, taking me into his arms to steal kisses, and groping the round of my butt. It's awfully strange how uninhibited he is. He's like a man with the hormones of a teenage boy. He's nothing like Adrian, who was always too angry with me for some reason or another to feel me up. Adrian probably should've broken up with me seven years ago, the year after I kept getting steady work. But as I stand here on the side of the road pressed up against Belmont, who pulls my hair to the side to nibble on the nape of my neck, which I've newly discovered is a hot spot, I can only blame myself for not being the one to break up with

Adrian seven years ago–especially if another man can make me feel this way.

"What are you thinking?" Belmont whispers thickly.

"I'm thinking that you must have more hands than an octopus," I joke.

It works. He chuckles. "Are you complaining?"

I shrug. "No, but… But you're making me…" I don't know how to say it out loud. I'm too embarrassed.

"Horny?" He's grinning mischievously.

"Yeah." I giggle like a girl with a crush. Actually, he makes me beyond horny.

Belmont is awakening me. I want to be sensual and sexual. I want to ignite his lust.

"I'm not trying to seduce you," he whispers as his hand snakes up and under my skirt. His fingers draw circles around my "ON" button. "I like to feel you quiver and twist. And those sexy sounds you make…"

"Are you a poet?" I sigh and chuckle.

And then suddenly he stops. I open my eyes in time to see a car speed by. Belmont lifts a hand at the driver, who honks back.

"Daisy," he says once we're alone, "I'm not going to touch you first again. You'll have to be the one to make the next move." He spins me around and draws my backside into him. I feel his chest rising and falling. "Starting"—he squeezes a handful of one of my breasts and then gently squeezes the nipple—"now." He's no longer behind me. He's beside me, his fingers interlaced in front of him, and smirking.

My body longs for his stimulation, but my mind is happy that it can finally focus. I let him fondle me with impunity, and I forget all the questions I must ask before I can truly trust him. A large part of me is still on guard.

"So it's Sunday, right?" I ask to get the ball rolling.

"Yep," he says, unaware of what's coming next.

"So do you work tomorrow?" I want to figure out what the heck he does on daily basis.

"Do we?" He smiles and does that flirting thing with his eyes.

Oh, he's smooth.

"Yes. I'm here to work, but what about you? What does a guy who goes to a nursery with a strange list of plants and then is directed to a strange house to buy pot do everyday?"

He laughs. "What makes you think I bought pot?"

"I'm sexually naïve, not generally naïve," I sniff.

"You're not sexually naïve. You're sexually neglected," he states. "And what? Do you think I deal drugs?"

I shrug. "Do you?"

He laughs harder this time. I seem to be delighting him somehow. "No, I'm not a weed peddler," he states for the record.

"Do you smoke it?" I ask slyly.

"Occasionally. Do you?"

"No."

"Never?

"Never. I don't ever want to try it. My body is my temple," I say with a smile.

He elbows me playfully and says, "You mean it's my temple."

I smack my lips and shake my head. "You just don't stop, do you?"

"It's true, Daisy. I'm going to enter you and worship you every day for the rest of our lives."

"You sound crazy."

"Crazy for you."

I burst out into laughter because that was not only corny but cliché. Even the dispenser of such tripe has to chuckle at that one.

"I wasn't buying weed," he says after our laughter simmers. "I bought an exotic tulip bulb. I hired a horticulturist to plant it for me. I put it in the glove compartment because I had to protect it from sunlight until it's ready to be planted, which is why I had to drive to Nancy's house to pick it up. She couldn't store it at the nursery."

"Really, what kind of tulip?"

"It's a mossy blood red bulb."

"Oh…" I'm embarrassed that I got it all wrong.

"So, Daisy," he asks in a completely different voice, "when are you going to make a move? I want to kiss you, but I can't because I'm a man of my word."

"I don't know." I shrug. "When the time is right."

"And this is not the right time?"

I narrow one eye to think. I shake my head. "No, I don't think so."

He laughs. "I see…"

"What do you see?" I'm grinning, so enjoying whatever game we're playing.

"You're playing hard to get. I've got to tell you, it's working."

"I'm not playing hard to get. You're just hornier than I am."

That gets another loud laugh out of him. "Only for you, babe, only for you."

"If every girl got a dollar for every time she's heard that…" I mutter cynically.

"You don't believe me?" He lifts an eyebrow.

I'm impressed; not many people can do the one-eyebrow-up trick. It makes him look even more scrumptious. "No, I don't."

"Fair enough," he says. "My actions will speak louder than my words."

I study his expression, searching for signs of inauthenticity. He is smiling as usual, but he doesn't look deceitful.

"You're going to kiss me now?" he asks.

I shake my head while still studying him. "You're right. I'm playing hard to get."

He runs a finger from my cheek to my chin and then steps back. "You sure are."

I face the main road. I haven't had much experience with men outside of Adrian, but I've been in ancillary relationships with my many girlfriends. I've watched them all make the same mistakes and listened to them complain and bellyache over the same incidences. My main take-away was sex clouds judgment, especially for a woman. Something about being penetrated makes the act so much more than just a casual one for the average, emotionally stable woman.

I've certainly had doubts about my love for Adrian. I used to ask myself if I even liked him. He was dull. Gosh, he's dull. I hated the way he name dropped as if he's best friends with all the Hollywood A-listers. It was way more tragic and sad when he tried to convince me—the woman who knew him best—that he was part of the in-crowd. He was annoying most of the time, but after we had sex, I felt as though I loved him more than any man on God's green Earth. The cycle of emotional deprecation will start all over again until I'm horizontal and he's on top of me.

That is why I will not make the first move. So far, I like everything about Belmont's personality, but I don't want the mind-blowing orgasms to make me miss something, especially in this early stage of whatever kind of relationship we're building.

"It's taking the cab forever to get here," I whisper, trying to suppress my lust.

"Where do you want the cab to take us anyway?" he asks.

"I don't know yet. I'll have to ask the driver."

"Ask the driver? What will you ask?"

"Maybe where's the most beautiful beach on the island?"

"Why couldn't you just ask me?"

"Because you're not a cab driver."

"He's just going to tell you what I can already tell you."

"Oh, Belmont," I groan, "you didn't call a cab, did you?"

He shows me his impish smirk.

"Belmont," I whine and slump my shoulders, pouting. "This is my article. Come on…"

"Daisy, the beach you're looking for is about a half mile up the road. And I read your articles. Maybe you should write a different kind of story. I don't see the cab-driver angle working on the Vineyard."

"You read my articles?" I'm stunned by that revelation. "When?"

"Yesterday after I dropped you off. I had a librarian friend send me some of your stuff. I read the ones on Antigua, Jamaica, Fiji, Aruba, Barbados, Provence and the French Countryside—"

"That's a lot!" I exclaim.

"What can I say? I'm a fan."

I roll my eyes. There he goes again, only this time I'm cheesing like a Cheshire cat. Adrian never read one of my articles. He always said that he didn't like to read about a destination before he got there, but once I caught him skimming a travelogue before his trip to Bermuda. A travelogue that wasn't written by me.

"All right, I'll do it. I'll forgo the cab and follow you," I say, swayed by the fact that he took the time to read my work before screwing me. That's certainly impressive.

"Really?" He seems surprised that I've given in so easily.

I bop my head, grinning. "Yes, and if I kiss you or something, then what does that mean? Do you get to make all the moves you want on me from then on?"

"That's exactly what it means." He smirks.

"Okay." I dig my heels into the gravelly drive and keep my arms at my side, determined not to submit to my own desires. "Then lead on."

He steps forward to stand nose to nose with me. He moves his face from one side of mine to the other. I forget to breathe, and when I remember, I release a long breath.

"I rarely like games, Daisy," he whispers, "but I like this one. I see that it's coming from an honest place." His lips are close to mine. "I want you to know"—his breaths beat upon my parted lips—"I'm not going to hurt you. You'll hurt me before I hurt you."

I gulp. "How do you know I'm afraid that you'll hurt me?"

"Because I pay attention." He steps back and takes a deep, calming breath. "Let's go before I declare myself the loser."

I can't speak; I can only nod.

On that note, he does an about-face. I sigh in relief one more time before following.

CHAPTER 6

The First Day of Ten Years

A quarter mile up the main road, we turn onto a trail. Dwarfed by the spiky forest of barely alive conifers and oak trees, Belmont curls an arm around my waist. The thistles crunch beneath my sandals and thick grains of dirt settle between my toes.

"The best part of the Vineyard are the beaches," he says like a good tour guide. "The hard part is getting to them. The public beaches are nice, but the best ones are hogged by property owners."

"You mean private ones?" I ask.

"Exactly."

"But I can't tell my readers to trespass. Are we trespassing?"

"Not if you're with me."

I glance up at him, amused, and his dancing eyes are already watching me. "So what do I write? Meet a local boy and he'll teach you how to trespass?"

"It's not hard to do. Especially if they look like you."

I drop my face and blush. "You're such a charmer."

"Do you know how beautiful you are?" He sounds serious.

"I'm uncomfortable with that kind of stuff," I admit easily and shrug. I've never said that to anyone.

"No, you're not."

"I'm not?" I ask, a little annoyed.

"Those are some very in-depth articles you wrote. Do you really think those cab drivers would've carried you around if you weren't so damn hot? What did you wear? The kind of dress you have on now? Or the red one from yesterday?" He bites his bottom lip as his mind wanders.

"You're just saying that because you are attracted to me. That's how it works. Attraction is subjective."

"Is that what you tell yourself?"

"That's what I believe," I say.

"That's what you choose to believe. Why is that?" There's nothing condescending or malicious in his tone, which makes it easier to answer his question.

I look up at him. He looks eager to hear my reply. "Who cares what I or anyone else looks like? In the end, it's the heart, spirit, and soul of a person that we're ultimately attracted to." I wait for his response, but all I hear are our footsteps and birds making peculiar noises around us.

"I agree," he finally says. He takes my hand and lifts it in front of his face. "It doesn't seem like we just met, does it?"

"No, it doesn't."

"I want to kiss your hand, but that'll be me making a move on you."

"That's true." I take back my hand playfully.

He tugs at the skirt of my dress. "When are you going to do it?"

"I don't know." I shrug. "Maybe on Friday."

"You really think I can wait that long? Hell, could you wait that long?"

"I don't know." I stare down at my soiled feet. "Maybe."

"I can't wait that long. I probably won't be able to wait five more minutes," he whispers. He looks at the ground as if the thought is burdensome. In a more spritely tone, he asks, "Were you an English or philosophy major?"

"Both, actually. Why you ask?

"It's what you said about subjective meaning."

"How do you know about it?"

"I'm an oracle, baby. I know everything." There he goes grinning again.

I shake my head, officially and once again charmed.

"All the hot girls were English majors, so I took a lot of classes I really didn't need," he confesses.

"Chasing girls in college, now that's a novel idea," I remark sarcastically.

"I bet you were being chased."

"No," I shake my head. "No, I was not chased. I'm sure of it. When I was in college, I looked like a twelve-year-old. I didn't blossom, really, until I was thirty-two."

"How old are you?"

"You're not supposed to ask a lady her age." I wink. "How old are you?"

"I'm thirty-five," he says.

"Ha! We're the same age."

"See, I told you. You and I"—he shifts his finger back and forth between us—"soul mates."

I gaze at the trail.

"Wait," Belmont whispers as he comes to an abrupt stop. He guides me to stand in front of him. "Look." He points out past a field of high grass that comes to a stop at the edge of a stagnant pond.

I narrow my eyes to see a little red ball perched on a broken tree stump.

"Is that a bird?" I ask.

"Shush," he gently admonishes me.

"It's beautiful," I whisper, heeding the warning.

It's a tiny bird about the size of my palm. Its skin is furry instead of feathery. I could literally pet it like a cat. As a matter of fact, that's exactly what it looks like, a brand-new kitten, only it's bright red and makes choppy, squeaking noises.

"Shoot," I curse under my breath. "I don't have my camera."

"How about this?" Belmont slides a cell phone out of his pants pocket and takes a picture. As soon as the camera clicks, the tiny bird leaps off the tree stump and flies away.

"Did you get it?" I ask him excitedly.

He holds the device in front of my face. In perfect zoom, clear and sharp, is the little red bird.

"Do you know what kind it is?" I ask.

He squints at the photo. "It looks like a Scarlet Tanager."

"Thank you," I mutter, trying to control the urge to fall back into his hard chest and let him do with me what he wills.

"You're welcome, but you're driving me crazy." He stands beside me and undresses me with his eyes.

"You can send that to me at my first name and last name, one word, at hotmail.com. Oh, and my last name is—"

"I know what your last name is," he says as if telling him would offend him. "I also know your email address."

I flinch, taken aback. "How?"

"Your online articles post your email address."

"Not my personal email address."

He lifts one eyebrow and smiles slightly. "You didn't let me finish." I'm enthralled by that sexy look on his face. "I wanted to read your article on the French Riviera, and I know the editor of Road W."

"You know Hunter Klein?"

He nods. "He's a good friend."

"Wow. What a coincidence."

His smile grows broader. "I know lot of people, babe! Which makes me an asset for you."

I pat him on the chest. "Always the charmer."

We gaze into each other's eyes for a moment.

"Are you going to kiss me now?" he asks.

I shake my head. "Not yet."

"All right then," he acquiesces. Belmont takes my hand and leads me on.

This part is all uphill, and we're back in the dense part of the woods. The weather is mild, but even though I'm panty-less and wearing a thin dress, I'm working up a sweat.

Belmont steps in front of me, leans over, and prompts me to hop onto his back. "Get on."

I hesitate, but he really doesn't have to tell me twice. I climb on and wrap my arms around his neck and legs around his torso. He totes me as if I'm a sack of feathers, which is surprising. Belmont has muscles, but he's still pretty lean.

"How much do you weigh?" he asks, testing my body mass by bouncing me.

I giggle because it feels as though I'm riding one of those mechanical bucking horses that used to be in front of grocery stores years ago. "I don't know."

"You don't know how much you weigh?" He asks incredulously.

I shrug against his back. He slides his hand down my thigh, massaging me. It felt so good. He really does have a sensual touch.

"You're about what, 5'8"?" he asks.

"5'7" and three-quarters."

"And you weigh about"—he bounces me again—"one-thirty?"

"I told you. I don't know. I've been too busy to care."

"Well, I'm here to tell you that you have a sexy-ass body."

"I believe I heard you say that already."

He laughs, and the next thing I know, he's pulled me off of his back. I'm wrapped in his arms. We're kissing so hard, and I somehow end up lying on the well-worn trail. We're going at it as if we're famished for each other. I'm whimpering and frustrated because I can't get past his flesh to merge with his soul.

Belmont fiddles with his pants with one hand and squeezes my breast with the other. I hear his zipper. He spreads my legs and stuffs his erection inside of me.

"Sorry," he whispers before his tongue dives into my mouth. He's thrusting me hard and fast and then nails me. "Damn..." He pushes deeper inside of me until his body quivers. He grunts in my ear. "Sorry, I couldn't wait," he says after he's fully released himself.

Then to my complete and utter embarrassment, two sets of legs walk past us. I let out a loud screech, grab his shirt, and bury my face against his chest. I hear giggling.

"Nice to see your ass, Jack," a guy says.

"It's nice and tight," a girl jokes.

I peak up to see Belmont throw up the middle finger, and the strangers laugh as they continue onward.

I cannot believe that just happened.

I remain mortified by what just happened all the way until we reach the edge of a grassy hill. The sight is breathtaking. A crystal-clear ocean stretches along the coastline and spreads to what looks like the edge of the Earth. The sleek, white sand shores that lie at the foot of steep, stony cliffs call my name. I tell Belmont he gets brownie points for taking me here.

"That's what I like to hear," he says and pinches my bare butt.

We gallop across the wild grass. Belmont scoots down the edge of a shallow hill and reaches up to help me to the sand.

"Take this off," he says, and before I know it, he's lifting my dress over my head. Then he drops his pants and pulls off his shirt.

We're as naked as jaybirds. "What? Is this a nude beach?" I ask, crossing my arms to hide my breasts.

"Yep." He takes my arms and moves them to my sides. Belmont can't seem to help himself from sucking on one of my nipples while he stimulates the other, and then he changes sides.

"No, let's swim," I whine. He's poking me with his poker again. He's like the Energizer Bunny.

"They're so brown and round... and real."

I shake my head, determined to not get screwed for a third time today. I step out of his grasp. One by one, I kick off my sandals. I look around. We're the only ones out here, so I run toward the water and dive in.

I'm a darn good swimmer. I used to be afraid of the great blue sea until one summer in Crete. I was lucky enough to join a group of tour guides on a training expedition. They rented a yacht to cruise the Matala coastline, and they spent all afternoon swimming the majestic Mediterranean Ocean. I was too afraid to join them until Javar Les, a sweet guy from London, took me under his wing and vowed to teach me how to swim and survive the sea. The hardest part was jumping in for the first time. After that, it was a piece of cake. For one week, we spent every day swimming the entire Greek Isle. Strong currents, smooth currents, deep, shallow—you name it, we swam it. Since then, I've been hooked.

The ocean is quite active, but I get control of my body fairly quickly. I flip over and try to float on my back, but the rapidly moving waves won't let me. Before I can flip back around, Belmont traps me in his grasp.

"I didn't know you were an Olympic swimmer," he says as we bob with the current.

He leans in for a kiss, but I shift out of his arms and swim toward a massive boulder rising out of the depths. As soon as I touch it, Belmont is right there, backing me up against the rock and pressing his lips to mine. It's a wet, slippery kiss. The boulder is in shallow water, so our feet touch the rocky surface.

"You like this?" he asks.

"I love it." I feel myself beaming as the thin waves crash against the rock and spray me in the face. "However..." I say after I'm able to see again.

The next wave slams into us harder, pinning me to the uncomfortable rock. Belmont twirls me around and leads us to shore. When we get there, he lays me down on the wet sand. He uses his knee to spread my legs and reaches down to stuff his hard-on inside of my sugar caves, but then suddenly he freezes. His narrowed eyes glare at something behind us. He rolls off of me and lies beside me.

"Shit," he gripes under his breath.

I lift up a little and turn to see what kept him from nailing me before I could think to stop him. A man, woman, and a dog are about twenty feet away, fully clothed and eyeing me specifically. It's as if they can't believe what they're seeing. I'm aware that my dress is laying too far away for me to run and put it on without giving them a healthy dose of my nakedness.

Belmont squeezes my bicep. "Relax."

"Are you sure this is a nude beach?"

"It's whatever kind of beach we make it," he says with his fingers interlaced behind his head while grinning from ear to ear. It's kind of weird how relaxed he is with his rod sticking straight in the air, choosing to stay erect until it gets what it wants.

I'm still up on my elbows, watching them. The couple tosses a Frisbee for the Collie to run and catch. They're no longer paying us any attention.

"Okay." I sigh and enjoy the cool water rolling in from the great Atlantic Ocean. I gaze up at the sky. I've experienced countless perfect moments on my many trips, however, this is the first time someone like Belmont has shared it with me. I can't believe the way I feel about him. Two days ago, my heart hurt so much I could hardly breathe. Now, I'm suffering the opposite of heartache. I could love him, I think as my eyes caress a white cloud streaking past us. Perhaps I could love him forever.

"So you operate charter during the summer and also work as a construction worker?" I really want to know more about him.

"I'm not a construction worker. I own a construction business," he says. He gently squeezes my nipple as though he's milking a cow. The sensation is distracting, but not so much that I abandon my objective.

"Then you build things?"

He pinches my nipple, and I whimper as he says, "Yep."

"Belmont?" I cover his hand with mine. "Take a break."

He chuckles and puts his hands back behind his head. "Go ahead, Daisy, continue the third degree."

I chuckle. "Charlie said your parents are dead."

"That's right." His eyes are closed. His hard-on is deflating, which is a clue that he's affected by that question.

I'm both relieved and disappointed. "I'm sorry to hear that."

He slides his thumb across my lower lip as he stares deeply into my eyes. "It's okay, babe." His voice cracks. "They died in a small-airplane crash."

"How long ago?"

"Six years ago."

I stroke his cheek. "I'm so sorry."

He seizes my hand and kisses the inside of it.

"You don't have to apologize. You didn't do anything, baby. If anything, you're making it all better."

I take in his beautiful profile. "Belmont?"

"Daisy?" His eyes are closed. He's stimulating my nipple again, and his penis is rising.

"Why don't you and Charlie like each other?"

"Long story."

"Long stories are too complicated to tell," I whisper, completely understanding.

We fall silent, but I feel his eyes on me. I look at him. He's watching me curiously.

"You're going to let me off the hook that easy?"

"If you don't want to talk about it, I can't force you."

"But it doesn't help my case."

I frown, perplexed, unsure what he means. "What case?"

"You're shunning the intimacy, Daisy. Make me tell you. I'm yours." My mouth is caught open. Belmont reaches over and pulls me on top of him. We're kissing, although not so deep that he can't talk. "Ask me what you want to know?"

"Okay then, what's the long story?" I whisper.

"Charlie's always resented me for being the older brother. He likes being on top." Suddenly he shows me a naughty grin and looks behind us.

"They're still around," I warn him and roll my eyes. Jeez, he's so insatiable.

The couple has ventured farther down the beach, but they're close enough to see him screwing me if he starts up again.

"We don't hate each other, Daisy. We're brothers, and that's never going to change."

He lifts me to my feet, takes my hand, and leads me across the sand to retrieve our clothes. Belmont helps me into my dress since my wet skin makes it difficult, and then he dresses himself. I hold my shoes in my hand as we trek across the shore.

"See that compound?" he asks. My eyes follow the direction he's pointing. A set of three houses, all identical, gray-shingled Colonials sit a safe distance from the ledge of the rocky cliffs.

"Nice," I say, thinking he's showing me a beautiful estate.

"That's where we're going—and Daisy?" He peeks at me carefully.

"Yes?" I sing as we pull up to a stop. It almost feels like he's going to ask me to marry him or something.

"I own that estate."

My eyes expand with surprise. "You do?"

"How about you stay there for the next two weeks? It's got a pool and some other great amenities. And the bed is really big and comfortable." He lifts one side of his mouth into a suggestive grin.

I take another look at the expansive estate. It surely is gorgeous. "But I've already paid six thousand dollars for the house I'm renting now."

"If you hadn't paid six thousand dollars, would you stay in my place?"

I shrug. "Yeah. Why not."

"Well, I called Epstein, who owns the house you're renting, and he agreed to give you your money back. He's already refunded your travel agent."

"What? When?"

"Yesterday. I had your things moved this morning." He looks worried.

"By whom? When?" I want to ask, "how," too but I know that will further stilt my already limited vocabulary.

"My housekeepers," he finally replies. "Are you angry?" He searches my face.

I look off into the horizon to think. I've never had this happen to me. He's trying to take over my life, and I love my independence! At least, that's what I used to think. What's wrong with me? Why am I not pissed off about this? Why am I turned on? Why am I not going to tell him to re-arrange all of his little arrangements and leave me alone you psycho?

Instead I sigh tiredly and say, "No, I'm not."

His lips stretch into a victorious smile. "Good. I was afraid you would knock me on my ass and tell me to go to hell."

"A) I'm not strong enough to do that, and B) I thought about it."

All of a sudden, his expression turns severe. "I would never lay a hand on you, Daisy." He smirks, grabs the round of my butt, and shoves it against him. "Wait, I take that back."

I chuckle at his not-so-corny joke. We kiss, and he's feeling me up. His hands squeeze me here and there and everywhere. It's as if he's not a man but an octopus.

"Shit, let's hurry." He sighs as he forces his lips away from mine.

"Wait," I say when he takes my hand.

"What?" His endorphins have him wild-eyed.

"What do you think about me beyond the sexual stuff?" I ask. I need to know the answer before I allow him access to my body again.

He studies my expression for a moment. Belmont's a pretty perceptive guy, so I'm sure he can see how desperate I am to hear his answer. "I don't know," he finally says. "You're still a mystery to me."

"I am?" I'm surprised to hear that. I thought I put myself out there for him.

"I can't read you. I'm falling for you really fast, and I don't understand why. Are you feeling the same way about me?"

"Yes," I must admit. "Which is crazy."

He wraps an arm around my waist and starts walking us. "So where are we going to live? I don't like L.A. The smog is bad, and traffic's a nightmare. Everything's crowded, and you can live in a place for an entire year and never see your neighbors once." His expectant eyes are shining.

"We're moving in together?" I ask, further surprised by his forwardness.

"Can you see yourself leaving here without me? Because I can't see it," he says.

"I don't know." I sigh. "I didn't think this would ever happen to me."

"Ah, now that's interesting. What did you think would happen if I hadn't come along?"

I take a moment to ponder that as we stroll along. "I thought I'd end up with Adrian for the rest of my life. Never married though. We both believed the ring, the minister, the church, and all the other shenanigans were unnecessary. Of course, he proved to be a lying hypocrite."

"I believe in all those shenanigans," he says, ignoring the part where I bitterly called my ex a hypocrite. "I want them with you."

I shake my head as I connect with my undeniable, innermost desires. "I don't think I could do it. I just don't believe in it. I wish I did, but I don't."

We turn quiet as we clomp through the sand. We arrive at a set of stone stairs. Belmont sits down and draws me onto his lap.

"Tell me more about yourself," he asks. He doesn't sound disappointed by what I revealed.

"Like what?" I ask.

"Tell me about your parents. Are they alive?"

"Yes, but they're divorced and married to other people."

"Any brothers? Sisters?"

"Two half brothers on my father's side and two half sisters on my mother's side."

"Are you close to them?"

"No, not at all."

"Why?"

I shrug. "It's probably my fault. I never make time for family. I spent the last three Christmases in Rome to capture the true spectacle of the season. And me and Adrian usually go somewhere together during Thanksgiving."

Belmont's entire face grows dim. "You gave him your Thanksgivings and he couldn't even give you a decent orgasm?"

I don't know how to respond, so I simply give him a tight-lipped smile.

He tilts his head. "You don't like to slam the people who hurt you, do you?"

"Not out loud." I chuckle. "But I think maybe I'm at fault too."

"Or maybe he's just an asshole who fucked your best friend behind your back."

"Maybe." I sigh dubiously.

"You're not at fault here, Daisy," he says with conviction. "If you worked too much and he couldn't deal with it, then he should've broken up with you. And he never read any of your work!" Belmont roars as if he's offended. "He'll be back, I guarantee it. What are you going to do when he comes knocking on your door?"

"I'm not answering," I say with a snarl.

He takes a handful of my wet hair and tilts my head back to kiss me. "That's what I wanted to hear," he whispers.

My head is spinning. Belmont stands and takes me with him.

We mount the stairs and he carries me piggyback across a grassy field. When we reach the wooden gate in a rock wall, Belmont fishes a clumpy set of keys out of his pocket.

"You have, like, a million of those," I tease.

He snickers and quickly locates the one he needs. He sticks it in the lock, but before he turns it, he strikes like a snake. He nails me to the wooden gate and shoves his hand between my legs. I pin my head to the wood as he does this two-finger thing to me. One is sliding in and out of me and one is circling my clitoris.

"Like that, baby?" he whispers as I whimper and pant against his lips.

"Uh hum," I moan.

"Me too." He bites gently on my top lip. "Come hard for me, baby."

"Daisy?" a high-pitched, familiar voice calls.

At first I think my mind is playing tricks on me, but then she calls again. Belmont and I freeze.

"Maya?" I call.

"What the hell's going on back there?" she asks.

My mouth falls open in shock, and I shake my head. Belmont removes his fingers from my nether regions and whispers, "To be continued."

CHAPTER 7

Confessions

*M*y eyes expand like a balloon. Never in a trillion years did I expect to see Maya here. But there she stands, looking like the adult version of a Bratz Doll in skintight skinny jeans, a tight pink tank top, and red stiletto heels. Her bone-straight hair trails over her breast implants, and she has on far too much makeup for the daytime.

"What are you doing here?" I ask. Contempt colors my tone.

"How do you know Jack?" She regards him as if she's starving and he's a cheeseburger.

"I asked what you are doing here," I nearly growl.

"I came to see you. We have to talk, don't you think?" I don't hear even a little remorse in her tone for the terrible thing she did to me. And she's still ogling Belmont.

I snap my fingers to claim her attention. "How did you even find me?" Gosh, I'm yelling.

"You're wet," she accuses. "Both of you are."

We're inside the compound, shadowed by bulbous oak trees. There's a sparkling, crest-shaped swimming pool in the middle of three structures, and to the right of it sits a white, wood gazebo with two lounge chairs facing the Atlantic. There's a lot more going on across the yard, but I'm too angry to take it all in.

Belmont curls an arm around my waist. We stand hip to hip, except his is higher than mine.

"I asked how you found me?" I demand.

"Leslie, our travel agent. I thought you were here to work."

"I am, and wow, that sounds judgmental."

"Then what are you doing here with Jack?"

"Again, judgmental." I glance up at Belmont. "And how do you two know each other anyway?"

She contorts her face into a kooky expression I've seen before. She does that when she feels she has a scandalous secret.

"We met through a friend," Belmont says. "Dorothy. Her boss."

"Yeah," she says with a cynical chuckle. "Dorothy."

"Something funny?" I hiss.

"No," she sings, which irks me even more.

"Does she know you're here?" he asks, glaring at her.

This is an odd moment. Maya rolls her eyes. Whatever cryptic message Belmont just sent seems to have done the job.

"Listen, Dais, can we talk?" She asks casually.

"There isn't anything else to say. You screwed around with and now you're marrying my ex-boyfriend."

She flips her long hair to one side and pulls the strands across her breast. She throws a glance at Belmont. She makes that move when she's trying to appeal to a man. The mere fact that a man's in the vicinity with his arm around me instead of her must be driving her nuts. "There's a lot to say," she says. Again, she eyes Belmont. Now I'm curious.

"Do you want her here or not?" Belmont growls, focusing only on me. So that's how he looks when he doesn't like someone. He doesn't even look at Charlie like that!

"Just give me five minutes, Dais, that's all," Maya pleads. "I owe you an explanation and so does Adrian."

My heart drops. "What do you mean, Adrian? Is he here too?"

"We just want to sit down and have dinner with you tonight. We're not leaving until you talk to us, so…" She shrugs as if saying no isn't an option.

"I don't care how long you stay because—"

"Maybe now's not the time for this," Belmont says, cutting me off. He looks into my eyes. "Let's talk about it, babe."

Maya flinches, taken aback. "Babe? Are you two a couple? If so, that was fast." I'm sure she couldn't wait to say that.

I ignore her. Maybe because she's the last person in the world I have to explain this unusual development to. "No. We don't need to talk about it because there's nothing to talk about," I reply to Belmont.

"I want to see this guy. I want to look him in the eyes and tell him there's no coming back."

"What? Why?"

"Wow... Jack and Daisy," Maya says as if she's trying it on for size. "Now that's an interesting pair."

Belmont and I glare at her. If looks could kill, she'd fall to the ground and choke to death.

"I'll make the reservation for four. Monarchy at seven," Maya says. Without a confirmation from either of us, she spins on her tiny heels and bobbles up the shell-covered walkway until she disappears down a narrow, tree-lined path.

My heart pounds like a jackhammer. What in the world just happened?

"Do you play checkers?" Belmont asks out of the blue.

"Huh?" I'm thoroughly confused.

"Let's talk over a game of checkers."

"But I don't know how to play." I'm frowning. My entire body aches. I want to run away, pack up, and go.

He knows Maya?

"I'll teach you," he says tenderly. He comes in for a kiss, but I lower my face.

"Whatever. Okay," I mumble.

"Hey..." He puts two fingers under my chin to lift my face. "I'm sorry all of this happened. I want to make it better. Will you let me?"

I want to ask him how in the world he plans to do that, but instead I nod. I go upstairs and hop in the shower to rinse the extra sand off of me. Unfortunately, I can't wash the mess my life is out of my head. Sometimes I wish I had an off switch, like in that movie Eternal Sunshine of the Spotless Mind. I would pay a million dollars to undergo that procedure. Maybe. I don't think I could ever want to forget Belmont Lord.

The ocean always dries out my hair, so I spread a conditioning mask on it while I shave the fine stubble off my arms, legs, and other parts. Keeping busy is the best way to forget all the crazy things happening in my life. After I rinse my hair and cut off the water, I towel blot and finger comb my curls.

I put on a casual, green, knee-length, long-sleeved, boat-neck jersey dress and warm, furry black boots. The weather is at least five degrees cooler than yesterday and steadily dropping.

"What are you wearing?" Belmont asks.

I jump. I didn't hear him enter the room. "This." I lift my arms to display my outfit.

He shakes his head. "It's too sexy. I won't be able to concentrate."

"You think everything I wear is sexy. This is not sexy."

"Really?" He sounds as though he's challenging me.

"Really." I fold my arms across my chest.

He walks over to me and squeezes my butt cheeks. "Ass." He squeezes my chest. "Tits." He looks at me as if that explains it all.

"You're crazy."

Suddenly I slam into his chest, and before I know it, we're kissing. His hands crush my butt, and he pins my lower parts against his hard knot.

"Let's get the hell out of here before I throw you on the bed," he claims breathlessly.

⁊ꙅ

We're in a black classic Thunderbird with the top up and the stereo off. I've noticed that he doesn't listen to music while he drives. Usually I had to tolerate Adrian's loud and weird instrumentals whenever I rode shotgun with him. He thought listening to strange indie music made him unique. Like Belmont, I don't listen to music when I drive. I can't think with all the background sound, and being alone in the car is the best time to plan.

There's a fair amount of traffic on the roads. Now that I'm sitting idle, my mind works overtime recalling the way Maya looked at Belmont. There was something familiar in her eyes, a look I'm trying to ignore.

"So…" I say to break the silence and stop thinking about Maya and Belmont together-together. "This checkers game is going to be a big deal."

He glances my way with a wink and a smile. "A huge deal."

"And you have to drive me to wherever we're going so that we can play checkers?"

"You mock me!"

"Yes, kind of."

He takes my hand and kisses my knuckles. "You can mock me anytime."

"What can't I do to you?" I twist in my seat to face him.

"Cheat on me," he answers right away. "I'll forgive you, but you would've ripped out my heart." Belmont doesn't take his eyes off the road.

"Don't worry," I say. "I'm not a cheater."

"You never cheated on your boyfriend?"

"Not once," I mutter, looking out the window. I recognize where we are. We're passing through Edgartown, taking a left at the fork to State Beach Road. "Have you?"

"I want to lie and say no, but I won't."

"Then you have." I actually don't know how I feel about that. Maybe he should've lied.

"After what that jackass did to you, that was probably the last thing you needed to hear," he says perceptively. "I can promise that I'll just leave before I cheat on you, and we'll sit down and talk about it before that happens."

"Talk about what? That you want to cheat on me?" I ask with a bite.

"A man doesn't cheat because he's an animal, Daisy. It really isn't how we're made. I know that for a fact. Fucking her and her and her eats away at your soul." A veil of sadness covers his eyes.

"I guess so." I sigh and gaze out the window at the Nantucket Sound. Shallow waves crisscross in the ocean, signaling that the wind has picked up. "It's just that he should've talked to me. I had no idea he was unhappy." I close my eyes. "Or maybe I did."

I wait to hear Belmont's response, but he remains silent. I face him. He's looking straight ahead and obviously has something heavy on his mind.

"How well do you know Maya?" I suddenly blurt out.

"I don't know her that well," he says defensively. "Met her a couple of times."

"Where?"

"Vegas."

"Did you have sex with her?" I ask. I know Maya well, and I saw the answer to my question in her eyes. I just want him to tell me I'm wrong.

Belmont squirms. "Once, and it didn't mean anything to me."

I want to cry. My sinuses swell, and tears are asking permission to roll. I clear my throat and swallow the condensation.

"I'm sorry if I just hurt you, babe. It meant nothing, really."

"Who came on to whom?" It's a crazy question, but I need to know.

"She came on to me," he says to my relief. He takes my limp hand. "Daisy, I didn't know she was the friend you were talking about. I think she's capable of doing what she did, but you and her in the same circle?" He shakes his head. "I would've never guessed it."

"Why not?" I wrinkle my eyebrows.

"She's into a lot of shit."

"Like what?"

He tenses, reluctant to answer. "You should ask her."

"Like she'll tell me…"

"She probably won't. I hate what she did to you. I'm not surprised. But she should tell you about it, not me."

"I remember she used to go to Vegas every weekend. She said she was seeing someone there. Was it you?"

"Hell no!" He lets out a long sigh. "Are we done talking about her? If I could take it back, I would. Especially if I knew I would meet you one day."

"Did you enjoy it–being with her?" I ask squeamishly.

"Nope."

"You're just saying that," I mutter.

"Daisy…" He glances at me. "I'll tell you the truth. If I had liked fucking her even a little, I would say so. I can give you the reasons why I didn't." He says that like he's waiting for a response.

I'm too curious to pass on the offer. "Sure, I want to hear it."

"You're tight; she's not. Chicks like her have this bone right here"—he pushes down on my pelvis—"that sticks you like a needle."

"All right." I throw up my hands. "I know I asked for it. I got it. No need to explain any further." I guess that was too much information.

"Are you sure?" He grins. "Because I have a lot more reasons."

"I'm sure you do."

We laugh.

He's still staring straight ahead. There's something satisfying about the conversation we just had; it makes me feel a lot better.

Belmont reaches over to stroke my thigh, and that's where he leaves his hand.

Oak Bluffs has an "Old Town" feel to it. It's quaint and cute but built for amusement. It hits us by surprise. One moment we're driving up Sea View Avenue, flanked by a pond on one side and a pristine ocean on the other, and then suddenly our attention is captured by a wide landscape of plush green grass. All the pathways cutting through Ocean Park lead to a white, wood gazebo.

Today, a wedding is taking place on the lawn. The guests are focused on the bride and groom, who are saying their "I do's" under the shade of the gazebo. The wind lifts the hem of her dress. She doesn't look too comfortable as she holds her floral headpiece in place with one hand. I bet she never predicted the uptick in the wind. That's the thing about the east coast; the weather can change like that. In L.A., ninety-nine percent of the time, the weather you wake up with is the same weather you go to bed with.

Belmont drives past the Oak Bluffs police station and stops at a sign. The general location looks familiar. I saw this all in my research on Martha's Vineyard. I identify the Flying Horses—which houses the oldest carousel in America—on Oak Bluffs Avenue and the tip of Circuit Avenue. The Campsite is not too far from here.

Belmont honks and the passing Jeep returns the beep. Instead of taking his hand off my lap, he lifts the one off the steering wheel to wave at the man in the white pickup. Soon he turns left into a famous community of gingerbread houses.

"Is this where we're going?" I ask, intrigued by the colors.

"Yep," he replies as he parallel parks, using one hand to navigate between two small cars without breaking a sweat.

"Impressive," I remark, grinning at him.

He leans across the seat, and I let him kiss me. Every time his tongue touches mine, my heart rate increases. His kisses are never casual; they're laced with passion and desire. My back straightens, and my chest puffs up as he pulls me toward him. He sucks on my chin and jawbone until he slides his warm, wet tongue down my neck. A moan escapes me. He's made me ready for whatever he wants to do to me next.

"Let's get the hell out of here," he whispers thickly.

Each gingerbread house is painted in a different color. Pink, blue, green, orange, red—you name it and it's probably splashed on one of those cottages. I feel as if we're traipsing through a neighborhood in a Brothers Grimm tale. Many have flowerbeds of tulips planted in front of the wraparound porches or sitting in flowerboxes on the rails. And then there are the domed bay windows that open to quaint balconies built into the gables. Frankly, I'm charmed by the entire spectacle.

Belmont takes my hand. He leads me up the dusty road and to a mint green cottage. He unlocks the door with one of his many keys.

"We're going in here?" I ask, surprised.

"Yep."

My awe is quelled as soon as we're inside. The entire ground floor is vacant. "There's nothing here," I say.

"We're going upstairs," he replies.

Belmont takes my hand and leads me up the stairs to a room with a bed, two big armchairs in front of a dome-topped bay door with a square table between them, and a ceiling that's so low Belmont can reach up to touch it.

"Give me a second." He gets on his hands and knees to dig under the bed. He says I'm sexy, but he's the sexy one. No one has ever made tan slacks and a light blue V-neck T-shirt look so appealing. And he's wearing a pair of white, blue and orange tri-colored designer sneakers on his feet. He's so well put-together, and it's a turn on.

"Got it!" he says victoriously and pulls out the game of checkers.

I'm still mesmerized by his sexy physique when he stands and takes the box to the table. He sits in one of the chairs and arranges the pieces on the board.

"You're red. I'm black," he says.

"Is that because red's for girls?" I ask, grinning.

"Exactly." He smiles back. "How did you know?"

"I have a brother."

"Oh, one of your father's sons? I thought you weren't close?"

"No, I'm talking about my older brother."

He lifts his eyebrows. "Where does he live?"

This is the hard part. My legs grow weak, and I sit down in front of the red pieces.

"He doesn't live anywhere. He's dead." I keep my eyes pinned to the board.

I feel Belmont's reaction in his pause. "I'm sorry. I can see how hard it is for you to talk about it."

I nod as my eyes water and sinuses constrict. I clear my throat to keep my voice from cracking in case he asks me another question about Daniel.

"This isn't going to work," Belmont claims.

The next thing I know, he takes my hands and lifts me to my feet. We shuffle around the table and he yanks my body against his. His tongue is deep in my mouth. Every part of him is rock hard: his thighs, his chest, his hands, and his rod. Belmont has a way of being forceful yet gentle. The way he shoves a hand under my skirt and squeezes is a perfect example.

"Do you have sex often?" He asks as the tips of his fingers slide in and out of my vagina.

"No," I gasp. "Why would you ask me that?"

"Because you're waxed."

"Oh," I sigh. "I like it. It feels cleaner." I let out another loud gasp when his fingers curl inside of me, and he pushes them against something. I have no idea what he's touching, but it creates the most pleasurable feeling.

"I know I'm taking a gamble and I'm asking a lot," he whispers. "But I want to see this guy, your ex."

"Huh?" I cry out as his palm shifts against my pubic bone and works in unison with his fingers. I'm on the verge of climaxing. I grab his shirt, clinging to him as he walks me to the foot of the bed and lays me down.

Belmont certainly has the magic touch. He knows how to take me from zero to screaming out of my head in less than ten seconds. That's exactly what I do until he wraps his tongue around mine. He snatches off my panties. As soon as he unbuttons and unzips his pants, his rock-hard erection springs forward. Instinctively, I spread my legs as he kneels between my thighs, staring into my eyes. I wonder what he's thinking. His lips are parted, and he's breathing heavily.

He touches me there and lifts his fingers to his nose. "I love the way you smell"—he puts the fingers in his mouth— "and taste."

There's nothing but fiery lust in his eyes. He peels me out of my dress and unhooks the clips at the front of my bra. He watches my breasts fall out of the cups.

"Daisy, he's not going to leave until he sees you. The faster he's gone, the better," Belmont says out of the blue.

At first I'm confused, but then it computes. "Adrian?"

"Yeah, your ex."

"Do you think we should talk about this right now?" I ask, panting from desire.

"I want him to see that you've moved on." He pauses to get a good eyeful of my naked body. "Hell, I don't know where to start first."

"Belmont," I say, way more sober than he is. I lift myself up on my elbows.

"Yeah?"

"Belmont," I call louder, hoping to rattle him out of his stupor.

He blinks hard. "Yeah?"

"Okay," I say. "I'll do it. I'll see what he has to say."

"Will it be hard for you to see him?"

"I don't know," I admit.

"Do you love him?"

"No, I don't."

"Do you love me?" he asks.

My mouth is caught open. Yes! my heart shouts. But then it tells me to beware. I usually lose what I love. Love has never been my best friend or made me any promises of happiness. For all general purposes, love has become my enemy.

Without receiving an answer, Belmont impales me with his thickness. Slowly, carefully, he thrusts. Our hearts beat near each other and our lips press hard against each other.

"Do you love me?" he asks again.

"So soon?" I whisper.

"Doesn't take long when it's like this." Suddenly he pushes deep inside of me, grunting and quivering. After a few moments, he becomes still. "See how fast that was?"

We both burst out in laughter.

"I already know how you feel about me," he says after we simmer down. "You wouldn't be here if you didn't love me."

"Is it love or lust?" I feel comfortable enough with him to ask hard questions.

"It's both."

"Or one."

He turns silent and so do I.

"We could test it by not having sex, but I've got to have you. I'm in lust with you. Can't deny it. But I love a lot of things about you too."

"Oh yeah, like what?" I doubt he knows enough about me to love a lot about me.

"You're gentle. I love the way your eyes light up when you're captivated by something, like the beach or a red bird. You look at me like that sometimes, and it gets me right here." He pats his chest. "And here." He prods me with his brand-new erection. He sighs as he continues thrusting me. "And you're smart. You're not cheap; you're expensive. I can't believe I can afford you. We're going to grow old and gray together. You watch."

I can't focus on all the reasons I feel the way I do about him because he withdraws his rod to trail kisses down my belly and latches onto my hot button.

An hour later, we lay together, loose limbed, on the bed. The checkerboard looms in the distance. Just seeing the perfectly placed pieces makes me chuckle at how easily we abandoned the plan. Belmont looks confused by my laughter.

"I thought we came here to play checkers."

"We did, and we will," he says optimistically. "One day. When this"—he waves a hand across our naked bodies—"calms down."

"You think we'll be together that long?" I ask before I can take it back.

Belmont lifts me on top of him. "Always doubting. Why is that?"

"What do you mean?"

He plants a quick yet meaningful kiss on my lips. "You just can't give in to this. You want to, but you can't. I think it's about more than your ex-boyfriend. I thought it was him until you told me about your brother."

"Huh?" I croak and scramble out of his embrace to sit on the side of the bed.

After a moment, he sits beside me. Our faces are very close.

"I'm not going anywhere, Daisy," he declares in an intimate voice. "You have to trust someone. Why not me?"

I close my eyes. "I trust people," I say unconvincingly.

"Is that so? Who might they be?" he challenges.

"My..." I start but stop. I want to say "parents," but this thing with Belmont makes me more honest with myself. I close my eyes and shake my head.

"It's okay, babe." He gently kisses my mouth.

"My parents divorced about a month after my brother died," I disclose.

He doesn't drawback or move an inch. He stays close, so close I can feel his breath upon my lips.

"It was like once he was gone, there was no need to be a family anymore. They both remarried, had other children..."

I don't realize I'm crying until one of my tears drops onto my thigh.

Belmont's lips go to work, kissing and licking the skin beneath my eyes. His tender act makes me able to give in to him fully. I accept his gesture, and my lips greedily seek his. Our arms and hands grasp for each other. Our legs twist and curl. I whimper as my mouth seeks refuge in his.

"Yes," I finally say. "I do love you."

CHAPTER 8

Unburied Secrets

*B*elmont and I leave the checkerboard alone. He says we'll come back tomorrow and play a few rounds. I certainly hope not. Since I've admitted that I don't think I matter to my parents, I'm contemplating confessing that I hate board games, especially checkers.

I glance at him as the colonial structures of his beachside estate come into view. It's hard to believe I'm in a relationship with the person who owns that cluster of houses. It's so permanent, so adult. And then there's Belmont himself. He's so perfect for me, and at first sight—or second and third sight— I would've never guessed it.

I didn't call Maya and tell her we're planning on meeting them at the restaurant. I hope that she and Adrian decided seeing me again was a lost cause and packed up and ferried out.

Belmont leaves me alone in an office to fire up my computer and work a little before we leave. Lo and behold, there's an email from Dusty. He's, checking up on my progress, requesting pictures and reiterating how excited he is about hosting an article for the taxicab series that I haven't yet begun to write.

I respond that I will get back to him in two days with photos and a teaser. Although to be honest, I'm not quite sure that will happen.

I also have three magazines requesting articles covering Peru, Mali, and cities around the Caspian Sea, which can be a little dangerous. Before all hell broke loose in my life, I would've said yes to Peru and Mali and probably to the Caspian Sea. I would've penciled each trip in my calendar, and they would've brought purpose to my life.

For now, I don't answer any of the editors yet. I need a few days to decide. I sit back in the black leather swivel chair and look out the window. What a nice office space. The sun has long set, so it's dark out, but yard lights illuminate the trees beyond the window.

Belmont is somewhere in the house when I decide to get up and get dressed. He sure does know how to give me space, and for that, I'm appreciative.

Funny, I can't get a song out of my head, and now I'm humming it. It's "Need You Now" by Lady Antebellum.

I make it to the bedroom. I strip out of my dress and decide to take another shower. The warm water rains down on my skin, and the steam encapsulates me. Now I've gone from humming to singing. I sound awful, but it doesn't matter. I love this song, and not even the water spraying my face can quiet me.

"Who, me?" Belmont whispers in my ear. His naked body rubs against my backside as his hands on my belly draw me into him. "If you need me now, then here I am."

I giggle like a teenager with a crush. My eyes are still closed when he spins me around to face him. "What are you doing?" I try to blink my eyes open.

"No." He covers my eyes. "Keep them closed."

"Why?"

He removes his hand, and I open them. "Trust me, Daisy." His dry lips kiss my moist ones. "Close them." He waits for me to do as he asks.

I concede with a deep sigh. Suddenly, the hand that has become as familiar to me as a third limb slides between my thighs. I step my legs apart.

"Don't move," he orders and prompts me to move my leg back where it was before. "No matter what I do to you, don't move."

I chuckle nervously. I figured Belmont was a sexologist, but he is quite naughty.

"You're slippery," he whispers heavily.

His hands squeeze my breasts, and then his teeth bite my nipple. I part my lips to release a gasp when I feel the sting. The throbbing is quickly replaced with a soft, sensual warmth. He does the same thing to the other breast, following the pain with pleasure. Belmont mutters something unintelligible as his hot mouth bites and sucks up to my neck. He's breathing hard through his nose as he sucks harder and harder.

And then there's nothing, only the water spraying my back.

"Open your eyes," he says, panting.

I open them immediately. He's staring at me, conflicted.

"What's wrong?" I ask. I would have thought he'd lost his desire to go through with whatever he had planned, but his erection is still pointing straight at me.

Without saying a word, he takes me by the waist and lifts my feet off the shower floor. Instinctively, I wrap my legs around him. We haven't broken eye contact.

He's shivering like he's cold as he inserts himself in me. I whimper because it feels so good.

"Shush," he pleads. "I want this to last."

I nod, making sure I don't make a sound. He doesn't shift my hips or his. This is the strangest moment ever.

"What's wrong?" I finally whisper.

"I want to be inside of you, that's all."

"Oh…"

"I think I'm going to lose you," he confesses.

I flinch, taken aback, and as soon as I move, his body jerks and he grunts, letting loose inside of me.

"Shit." He shakes his head. "I don't know what the hell's going on with me when it comes to you."

"It's okay." I try to sound consoling. I unhook my legs to stand on my own two feet, but he lifts me higher, signaling me to put them back.

Belmont opens the shower door, carries me out, and walks us to the bed. He lays on top of me. "You're on the pill?"

"Oh, now you ask."

He plugs me once, twice, three times with his brand new, hardening erection. We grin at each other.

"Yes, I am," I answer. "Although I never tested its potency to this extent. Heck, I hadn't had sex in three months before you came along."

He kisses me. "Happy I could oblige."

I sniff, chuckling.

"We could do it you know." His eyes are all alight.

However, my eyes widen in horror, knowing exactly where he's going. "Do what?"

"Have a kid. You and me."

I grunt and try to wiggle out from under him. He jabs me with his penis a few more times, and I end up holding on to him again.

"You don't want to have children?" he asks after he's regained control of me.

"Why are you asking me this when you're inside of me injecting me with baby-making juice?"

He laughs out loud. "'Baby-making juice.' I never heard that before!"

"Well that's what it is. And you know the pill isn't a hundred percent, so we should be careful. Especially in six days."

"What's happening in six days?" There he goes prodding me with his penis again, sliding in and out of me slowly, indulgently.

"I think I ovulate."

"So we have six days to fuck non-stop."

"Stop it," I say with a moan.

"Do you really want me to stop?"

There he goes, knowing exactly where he's poking me.

"No, don't stop doing that. Stop talking…" I whisper.

He stabs me in that spot and rotates his hips. I whimper as that sensation stirs inside of me.

It's coming…

I try to grab the sheets, but they're not strong enough. My hands clamp around his hilly biceps. That does something to him. His hips move faster, and he stabs me harder.

"Come for me, baby," he coaxes me. "Feel it… Do you feel it?"

"Yes," I screech.

"I can feel you tightening around me," he says breathlessly as he continues his relentless attack on that spot. "You like this?" He reaches under to grab my butt, and he shoves me into him.

Suddenly I experience the explosion. It's severe and saturates my entire nether region. Belmont doesn't release the pressure until long after the feeling subsides.

I'm breathing heavily when I open my eyes. He stares at me, smiling and satisfied. As soon as I smile back, he shoves deeper inside of me, thrusting and thrusting until he lets go in his usual dramatic fashion.

Once he stills, he flips me around to lie on top of his chest. I close my eyes to listen to him breathe. I'm safe in his arms and completely relaxed.

We lie like that for a while. My skin is drying, but his body is so strong and warm. He wraps his arms around me, still inside of me, and I melt like butter against his chest.

"Daisy!" Belmont's body quickens. He rattles me out of the sleep I fell into. "It's seven!"

We both hop out of bed. He rushes to call the restaurant to let Maya and Adrian know we're on our way.

I get dressed, but there's no time to be meticulous. However, I can never go wrong with my black-and-white, polka-dot, cap-sleeved Dior dress. Instead of twisting my hair into a tight bun like I usually do when I wear this dress, I fluff out my already puffy mane. It's been duly noted that Belmont likes it this way. I slip my feet into a pair of red, ankle-strapped Sergio Rossi sandals.

"Whoa, you look like a million bucks," Belmont says when he walks into the bedroom.

He once again takes me by surprise. He's not big on announcing himself or knocking, and I'm shocked that it doesn't bother me. I love seeing his big smile and bright hazel eyes. I'll never stop loving the way he looks at me.

"Thanks to the consignment shops in the East and West Village," I say, showing off the Dior.

"I like that about you," he says, revealing the thought behind his admiring smile.

"What? That I chase down big-name labels in the consignment stores of Manhattan"—I dip my head to one side— "Paris, Milan. There are some really good ones in London too. Oh"—I lift a finger because I almost forgot—"and of course L.A. But the best ones are in New—"

I can't finish the sentence because he draws me against his body. Note to self—he likes pulling me into him.

Almost ceremoniously, he puts his lips against mine. "Um, you smell good," he whispers once our lips part.

"By the way," I whisper, "you look really good too."

He has on a camel-colored vest over a crisp white button-down shirt. His gray, pinstriped trousers fit him like they would a male runway model. I never noticed this until now but his legs are slight bowed. Goodness, he's so sexy.

"Thank you." He smiles.

"We fit." I grin.

"I'm not surprised."

"You know, that's a big plus in my book. I like a sharp-dressed man."

He chuckles, but there's a sensual ring in his tone. "Let's get the hell out of here before I rip that dress off you and throw you on that bed."

I gasp, feigning offense. "If you rip this dress, then you'll have to buy me a new one."

"I'll buy you a dozen." He kisses my top lip. "A red one…" He kisses my bottom lip. I smile harder. "A green one…" He kisses my top lip again. "A yellow one…" Our tongues wrap around each other. He sighs long and deep, grabs my hand, and walks me out of the bedroom.

Once we're on the road to Edgartown, I let Belmont know that tomorrow, I want to roam the grounds alone to get some shots of the property. He insists on giving me a tour, but I adamantly decline. I can't work and have sex with him every five minutes. He's too insatiable, and I have a job to do. He says he knows all the secret spots around his house and they'll be interesting details to add to my article.

"Can we have sex in those spots?"

I watch him with my eyebrows lifted.

"All right," he relents. "I get your point. I'll give you a map. I have work to do anyway."

"Really, work?" I feign shock. "You work?"

He chuckles. "Every goddamn day, even on the weekends. I'm sure the guys are wondering where the hell I am. At the moment, I'm building six houses on the Vineyard and two in Nantucket. And that goddamn retreat in Aquinnah is killing me." He glances at me. "Your presence has distracted me."

"Well, yours has distracted me too. Heck, I came here to write a story."

We fall silent. I gaze out the windshield. The wind has picked up and is blowing the trees westward. Stupid me didn't bring a sweater or coat. I would've remembered if I had gone outside, but I entered the car from the well-insulated garage.

"I want you to stay here with me. Don't go back to L.A. That city is shitty anyway," Belmont says.

I turn to study him, wondering if he's lost his mind. "Are you serious?"

He makes a right onto Main Street. "I am." He makes a left on Church and then a right down a small alley. He parks in a large, nearly empty parking lot.

"But my life is there," I mutter, studying my hands in my lap. The engine turns off. I feel his eyes on me.

"Your life is wherever you are." He shows me that million-dollar grin and winks.

"Let's just see," I say, offering a momentary compromise.

"It's not a flat-out 'no,' so I'll take it."

I feel as though I'm walking on air as we head to the restaurant. I ponder leaving L.A. Other than Adrian, there's nothing for me there. My dad lives in Windsor Hills with his new family, and my mom lives in Pacific Palisades with hers. They're both busy with their other children and their jobs.

He's a music producer, and she produces prime-time television. They work hard and long hours and as a result they were the ones who taught me how to be a workaholic.

I see them every now and then, but usually it's on a holiday like Christmas, and our reunions are very awkward. I've never voiced it, but watching my new brothers and sisters upsets me. I can't stop myself from feeling that in real life, none of them should be here. Daniel, my brother, should've never been hit by that car. I should've never witnessed his body flying high in the air and then slamming down on the concrete, breaking his neck and killing him instantly. Every time I look at my new brothers and sisters, all I see is Daniel, eyes wide open, watching me as if he's apologizing over and over again for leaving me alone in this world. Maybe that's why packing up and leaving the city pains me. His soul still lives there at 6556 Poplar Avenue.

"A dollar for your thoughts," Belmont says when we reach the crowd of people in front of the restaurant waiting to be seated.

I put a quick kiss on his lips. "I'll tell you later."

He doesn't let me go that easily. In front of all those eyes, he lifts my chin to kiss me long and deep.

I try not to look at anyone when he opens the door because that kiss was a little too much for public consumption.

"They're already seated," he says after clearing his throat.

Across the room, eyeing us intensely, are Maya and Adrian. He's scowling and I'm sure, like everyone else, he saw the sensual kiss that Belmont just laid on me through the window. The restaurant is not very large, nor is it tiny;

115

it's intimate. Maya and Adrian are seated near the wall, away from the center of the floor. I imagine they asked for privacy. When we get to the table, Belmont pulls my chair out for me.

"Pretty dress," Maya says as I sit.

"Thanks," I mumble and look at her.

She's wearing an aqua-blue, one-shoulder, skin-tight number. Although she's seated, I'm sure it's just as short as it is fitted. She doesn't mind showing her crotch to the entire world. Tonight, she's wearing pink lip gloss and blue eye shadow above a smoky eye.

"You too," I lie, and it's pretty evident I'm being disingenuous.

Adrian, on the other hand, is wearing an off-white cable knit sweater, and I don't have to see them to know that he's also wearing a pair of gray trousers. I've seen the outfit many times. I also know what he's going to order and that the drink in his glass is scotch on the rocks.

"Don't need to ask how you're doing," Adrian mumbles spitefully. He shoots Belmont a dirty look.

"I'm fine," I say anyway, and I try to sound respectful. He looks upset that I'm happy, which makes me want to rip off his face. What a jerk.

"And you, Jack?" Adrian spits and turns up his nose disrespectfully.

I frown, wondering why in the world he is calling Belmont Jack. Then I realize that Maya must've told him that's his name.

"It's Belmont," my lover corrects.

Adrian sniffs dismissively. "Whatever."

Maya's eyes dance as if she's enjoying the entire exchange.

"So, I'm here," I say forcefully enough to claim the group's attention. "What do you want to say to me?"

I focus on Adrian in particular. Adrian scrunches his lips as if he's refusing to speak.

"We wanted to apologize," Maya offers and touches Adrian's shoulder.

He turns his shoulder away from her like a pouting child who doesn't want to be touched by his mother. "I was sorry, but I'm not anymore. Why are you with this guy, Daisy?"

"Hey, cool it," Belmont growls, ruffling his eyebrows.

"Why are you with her?" I ask, stabbing a finger at Maya. "What I want to know is when did you, and you"—the finger shifts appropriately—"start screwing each other?"

"You know we were over a long time ago, Dais."

I thrust my body forward in his direction and my sternum slams into the table. "Then you should've said that. You should've said, 'This is over, Daisy. I'm done, Daisy. Let's go our separate ways for good.' Not, 'Let's take a break.' That implies you'll be coming back, not ending up engaged to my ex-best friend."

Maya butts in, "No, we'll always be friends." She sounds very sure of it.

I shake my head and glare at her. I can't believe she said that. "Really, I would be the turtle who carried the scorpion across the pond if I continued to have any association with you."

Maya and Adrian appear shocked. They're not used to seeing me all worked up like this. I've always been passive. Being with Belmont has helped me realize that my indifference was merely another brick on the wall I'd erected between me and anyone who sought to get close to me.

A young waitress steps up to the table to take our order. "Hey, Belmont." She blushes.

"Hi, Amy," he answers. I can hear the stress in his voice.

Maya snickers. "You're popular with the ladies here too, Jack."

Belmont narrows his eyes at her. "You want something to drink, babe?" he asks me as calmly as possible.

"Whatever you think is good," I mutter through clenched teeth.

"'Babe'?" Adrian repeats sarcastically.

"What do you care?" I snap. I aim my finger right at Maya's head. "You're here with her. Why are you acting this way?"

"You never gave a damn about being with me anyway, Dais," he says frankly.

What a way to make himself the victim. "You're such a self-centered jackass," I say as though it's the saddest thing in the world.

The poor waitress watches us as if we've all gone insane. Belmont takes my hand to remind me that he's here and I'm not alone.

"Don't touch her, man," Adrian has the nerve to say.

Belmont rips his seething eyes off of Adrian. "Amy, won't you give us a minute?"

"Okay," Amy says with trepidation.

"Let's go outside," Adrian says, glaring at me. "I want to talk to you alone."

"No." I fold my arms defiantly. "I'm not going anywhere with you."

"Do you even know who this guy is?" he asks.

Maya elbows him. "Shut up, Adrian."

"Do you want to apologize to me or not? Because if not, we're done here," I hiss.

"We wanted to tell you that we never meant to hurt you," Maya says with carefully composed control.

"This dude"—Adrian points his chin at Belmont—"is a gigolo. Did you know that?"

Wow, I mouth. "You're willing to stoop that low… Lying does not suit you."

"You don't believe me?" Adrian sneers. "Ask him." He glares at Belmont. "Didn't Maya pay you to fuck her?"

I'm waiting to hear Belmont deny it and punch Adrian dead in his wimpy mouth. When he doesn't say anything and Maya's eyes flicker—as if she's pretending to be shocked—I whip around to look at Belmont. He's watching me, seemingly tongue-tied.

"I'm sorry, Jack," Maya says. "He wasn't supposed to say anything."

"Is it true?" I ask Belmont, nearly shouting.

He looks at me as if he's swallowed a snake, and I know it's true. The past two days crash down on me like a love nest made of straw. I want to crawl into a hole and hide.

"You just couldn't let me have this, could you? It's so funny that everyone we know warned me about you. Stupid me for choosing to give you the benefit of the doubt," I snap at Maya, who orchestrated this moment. I shoot to my feet.

I turn my anger on Adrian. "And I should've never gotten involved with you, ever."

"Daisy, I don't want to hurt you. I love you," Adrian says desperately.

Maya flinches, taken aback as if hearing his confession is news to her.

"You sure have a funny way of showing it," I whisper, resigned to the fact that my life has been ruined. That pain in my chest has returned with a vengeance. I need cold, crisp air—Adrian-, Maya-, and Belmont–the-Gigolo-free air.

I think I'm walking. I hear more than one person call my name. The door is so close, and I pull the handle to open it as though my next breath depends on it. My tears roll freely. There's nothing I can do to stop them, and I don't want to stop them. I'm embarrassed and ashamed of myself. I stepped right into Belmont's trap, and Adrian and Maya couldn't wait to tell me. He's a liar. They're liars. I need to get off this island.

"Daisy!" Belmont shouts. His hand squeezes my bicep, and he pulls me into him.

"Let go of me," I huff, jerking out of his grasp.

He does as I ask and lifts his hands to show me he's complying. "Let's go home. We can talk there."

"Home?" I snarl. "That's right. I should go home."

"No, you're not leaving the island. Not like this."

A couple holding hands walk past us. They're being nosy. I've never been the sort to make a public scene. Then I see Adrian and Maya walk out of the restaurant.

"Okay, just get me away from here," I implore. Belmont doesn't have to be told twice. He tries to take my hand, but

I pull away. I refuse to acknowledge the pain in his eyes. "I don't want to walk past them."

Maya and Adrian are headed in our direction, and we'll have to pass them to get to the car. Belmont reaches for my hand again. I let him take it this time because I trust him to get me out of here without running into the people who have singlehandedly destroyed my life.

We turn left at the next road and nearly run up an alley. Swimming has given me very good endurance, so I can keep up with him as we sprint to the car. Belmont and I stare miserably into each other's eyes as he opens the door to let me in.

He drives slower than usual. I stare out the window, turned away from him. The night is as bleak as I feel.

"Daisy." His whisper disturbs the silence. "I wanted to tell you. I really did."

"You should've," I say after a long pause.

Charlie's comment about Belmont being good in bed makes sense now. And he is good! He's an expert. The things he's done to my body. And then I wonder... "Do you have a sexual addiction or something?"

"Huh? No!" he replies, disgusted. "You know what I think?"

"What?"

"You're making more of this than you should because you want me to hurt you."

"Ha," I scoff. "You lied to me and now you're accusing me of overreacting?"

"I used to be a gigolo. The operative word is 'used' to be."

"But you used your sexual tricks to make me think I loved you."

121

"If you love me because I made you come, then you really didn't love me at all."

"Maybe I don't. I wouldn't know. I just..." I close my eyes and massage the tension at the bridge of my nose. "I just want to be somewhere else right now."

The car makes a swift right turn and comes to a screeching halt along the side of the road.

"Don't leave the Vineyard, Daisy," he pleads.

I watch him, tongue-tied. Even now, I find his face attractive, but I can only see him as another man that Maya screwed who claimed to love me. At least he confessed that he had sex with her. He just left out the part about how she paid for it. There's something iniquitous about that whole ordeal.

"How long has it been since you've worked as a...?" I ask quietly while staring straight ahead.

"Five years, three months, and thirteen days," he whispers.

"Why did you do it? Aren't you from money?"

He sniffs disdainfully. "I didn't do it for the money."

"Then why did you do it?" I sound so sad.

"It's a long story, Daisy."

"Then you should start talking."

He studies the way I'm looking at him. After a moment, he chuckles. I'm wondering what's funny when he says, "I must really love you if I'm going to dig up this shit out of the landfill."

I frown, conflicted. Belmont strokes my cheek with the back of his hand.

"After I graduated from college, I left Denver and moved to L.A. to become an actor. I figured I had the looks, the personality; hell, they'd be knocking down my door." He smirks nostalgically. "It took me seven years to learn I didn't have any goddamn talent. But I kept getting auditions. The casting couch swings both ways."

"What do you mean? Are you bi-sexual?" I ask.

"No, babe," he replies quickly. "There are a lot of power-ful women in Hollywood. Some men tried with me, but I was just never into that."

"So what–these women paid you to sleep with them?"

"Not directly. I got auditions, small parts. I could never hold the job because I'm a horrible actor."

"When are you going to get to the gigolo part?"

He sighs and looks into my eyes. "I've lost you already, haven't I?" He sounds so sad.

I shrug. "I don't know, Belmont. I need to process this."

He nods as his eyes gleam with hope. "That's fair."

"Are you going to finish telling me?"

"You still want to know this shit? Why?"

"Because I want to know everything about the person I fell in love with in such a short amount of time."

"Remember that."

"Remember what?"

"That you love me."

His expression is so sincere. I nod. "I will."

"Okay," he says as if I've given him permission to con-tinue. "I was with a woman who said I was fucking up her reputation and making a fool out of myself by auditioning. She said acting wasn't my talent–making women feel—" He stops cold turkey.

"Loved," I mutter. My chin quivers, and it doesn't want to stop trembling.

"I love you, Daisy. Everything I said, what we did, none of it was an act. Remember, I'm a terrible actor."

"I'm so hurt," I whisper. I sniff and wipe the tears off of my cheeks.

Belmont squeezes my hand. I don't withdraw it because I can't move. I'm not numb, but I want to be.

"Don't just pack up and leave. Promise me you won't. If you decide that you have to get the hell out of Dodge, tell me first," he says.

"Okay," I acquiesce. I'm exhausted and need to be alone. "But I can't stay in your house?"

"Yes, you can, and you will. I'll go across the street, give you time to cool down. When you call me, I'll come right over. And I won't come over until then."

That's how we leave it. Belmont drops me off and doesn't come inside. I can tell it kills him to watch me leave without him, but I can't be with him right now. I need space. If he touches me, I'll let him make love to me because I love him.

I curl up in a ball on top of the bed without undressing or washing off my makeup. Even though my stomach growls and my head hurts from hunger and heartache, I close my eyes and let exhaustion put me to sleep.

CHAPTER 9

A Change in Direction

When I wake up, my whole body aches. Some of those pangs are from swimming, some from the sheer amount of sex I had in twenty-four hours, but most are from the events of last night. I would think it was a horrible nightmare if I wasn't still wearing the Dior.

I hug myself because it's cold. I look out the window. The day is gray and cloudy. It's not raining now, but the window is wet from earlier rainfall. Good thing I packed for abrupt weather changes. Yesterday's rough waves were a clue that wind and rain were coming.

I scoot off the bed, carefully take off my dress, and fold it away. I'll take it to the cleaners as soon as I get home. I feel how wild my hair is, so I rush to the bathroom to tie it up into a big, fluffy ponytail. Then I do the one thing that always relaxes me–take a bath.

The bathtub is extremely ostentatious. It's behind the wall with the double sinks. I have to step up two platforms to get to it. Figuring out that there's a remote control to turn the water on and off and to set the temperature takes me a minute.

I program a warm bubble bath and don't have to wait long for the tub to fill. It's perfect–about the only thing that's gone right recently.

I'm no longer hurt by what Adrian and Maya did. Good riddance to both of them. I wonder what she's going to do now that her fiancé has said he still loves me. I can hardly believe he played that card. I'd never go back to him, especially not after learning how crummy he is in bed. It's not only that though. Belmont read a whole slew of my articles in one afternoon, and Adrian never read one. Belmont pleaded for me to stay; Adrian wouldn't have done that.

"What's my problem?" I whisper and close my eyes.

Why do I want space from Belmont? Could he be right? Am I looking for a reason to run away? Am I more comfortable being alone?

Adrian was right to be frustrated by our relationship. If my career had gone bust, then we probably would've broken up a long time ago. I think we used to see each other five days a month. Ten days on a good month. The more time I spent with him, the more I disliked him. The less time I spent with him, the more I liked him.

I don't want to run away from Belmont Jaxson Lord, but he was a gigolo who screwed Maya. I sigh at that thought and the fact that we've been having unprotected sex. "Stupid me." I pound myself in the forehead with my palm.

"Hey, sexy."

Caught off guard, I turn to the doorway, making sure my nakedness is well hidden under the bubbles. "What are you doing here, Charlie?"

"Can I join you?" He grins mischievously.

"Absolutely not!" I look for my towel just in case I have to grab it. "Who let you in? Does Belmont know you're here?"

"Yes, he does." Charlie leans on the doorway. "I kind of feel sorry for that fucker. What did you do to him?"

"Nothing," I say defensively.

"You found out, didn't you? His deep, dark secret."

"Yeah," I whisper dejectedly.

We fall silent. I notice Charlie is looking at me differently than before. There's something in his eyes that wasn't there before.

"I think I gave you the wrong impression," he says. "I don't hate my brother."

"I know. He told me that you two don't hate each other."

"We don't," he concurs. "Did he tell you what he did for me?"

"No."

"After our parents died, we got it all, split down the middle. I invested in the bubble, and when it burst, I had shit left. Jack gave me enough cash to start over, but I had a million-dollar habit."

"A drug habit?" I ask.

"Blow. I'm six months out of rehab," he says. "I was wrong to come on to you that strong. He's into you. So what if he had a swinging dick?" He smiles as though that was supposed to be funny. "Come on, lighten up. I'm backing off, but I still think you and I would make a cool couple."

"You think?" I ask sarcastically.

"Hell yeah! We'll be, what do you call it, contemporary, post-modern."

This time he gets to me, and I chuckle.

"I'll pounce on you like my brother does, but I'll show you a good time too."

"What are you doing here, Charlie?" I ask. It sounds like he's coming on to me again.

"I'm taking you out!" he sings.

"What?"

"I'm your taxi driver. Jack said I should show you around since he can't."

"No, he didn't."

"He said to give you time to walk around the grounds and take pictures and then to take you to Menemsha and Aquinnah."

I study him with one eye narrowed suspiciously. I think he's telling the truth. The part about walking the grounds is dead on, although I never believed Belmont would let me do it alone. He would probably show up at some point and seduce me with his sensual touch–his talent.

"Well… let me finish my bath first."

"Go ahead." He folds his arms and grins.

"Get out, Chuck."

"Oh, she called me Chuck. Belmont's rubbing off on you."

I shake my head, thoroughly charmed.

He backs up behind the wall and is gone. Suddenly, it makes sense. Belmont would rather subject me to Charlie than let me leave the island. This is his way of keeping an eye on me. He knows I'd never betray him by giving in to his brother's advances.

I don't rush my bath because the water feels like warm velvet on my skin. I could live in this tub. Close to an hour later, I get out and wash off last night's makeup without reapplying since I decide to go barefaced today.

Charlie has been waiting long enough, so I slip into a pair of faded blue jeans and a blue T-shirt with "Air Pollution Stinks" written across the front. I put on socks and shove my feet in a pair of water-resistant shearling boots. I grab my short black trench coat, camera, utility bag, and writing tablet, and I rush downstairs.

"Charlie?" I call once I reach the foyer. I open the door. My rental car is parked in the driveway and my keys are hanging on a hook by the door.

"One second," Charlie says on his cell phone. He puts his hand over the mouthpiece as he skips up the steps. "Daisy, I can't go. Got to go."

"Oh," I say. I sound disappointed, but I'm pretty much relieved. "Where to?"

He winks while turning his lips up into a naughty smile. No doubt it's an opposite-sex ordeal he's running off to.

"See you in a minute," he tells the girl on the other end of the call. "Brought your car back." He points to the Mini Cooper.

I nod.

He studies me and shakes his head as he skips back down the steps. He turns to face me. "So that's it?"

"What's it?"

"You're going to let me go just like that?" So funny, that's the same question Belmont always asks. What sort of neurotic women do they normally deal with?

"Why shouldn't I? If you have other things to do, then I don't want to get in the way."

"You really don't like me?" he asks with a high note of curiosity.

"I like you," I reply casually.

"But not like you like Jack?"

I part my lips. I want to confess out loud that I love Jack. I just hate that he's part of everything that went wrong. He's connected to Maya, and she used him to kick me in the other knee.

"No. Not even close," I whisper past my tightened throat.

Charlie nods and I can tell by his expression that that stung. He holds up a hand. "See you around, Daisy." He trots up the driveway and disappears in the brush.

That was strange, but I shake it off. It's time to plot my schedule for the day. When my stomach growls, what's first on the list becomes apparent.

The humongous stainless-steel fridge is stocked with all the groceries I bought at the Stop & Shop and a whole lot of other food. After locating the pots and pans, I whip up scrambled egg whites, brown some toast, and fry up some real bacon. Then I chuck it down as fast as I can. When I'm anxious to get to work, the hours in a day turn unconquerable. I also take out a salmon steak to broil for dinner tonight.

I wanted to take pictures of the estate, but it simply reminds me of Belmont. Instead, I go upstairs, turn on the computer, and find the phone number for a taxicab company.

The driver says he'll be here in ten minutes. I'm a little disappointed that Belmont hasn't called or texted. He hasn't even emailed the picture of the little red bird. He said he'll let me make contact with him first and he must've meant it.

As I sit on the stoop waiting for my ride, I wonder if I'm irked by the fact that Belmont used to get paid to have sex with other women. The answer is no. I'm not so judgmental. Really, I'm not. I'm more ticked off that I had to hear it by way of Maya's well-orchestrated plan to humiliate me for a second time. The first time was her post on Facebook.

After five minutes on the dot, the cab pulls up and catches me with my face lifted to the sky. I wonder when or if it'll rain again today. I love rain, and the east coast variety is one of my favorites. It's not misty and soft like a California rain. It's tough and has character. It's temperamental and unpredictable, like the region itself.

The driver gets out and opens the back door. I gather my things, make haste to get to the car, and scoot onto the seat.

"Did you say you were going to Menemsha?" he asks in a thick New England accent.

"Yes," I reply.

"Where to?"

"Do you know Menemsha well?" I ask, getting ready to work my magic.

"Yeah, I do," he says confidently.

"I'm a travel writer, and I don't want to waste my time showing people what they already know. Do you know somewhere off the beaten path that might pique my interest?"

"I can drop you off at the hills. You can walk the trails," he suggests.

"How long would it take?"

"As long as you want."

"I see." That's an indulgent leisure activity. "Well then, that's where I want to go."

"It might rain, though," he warns me.

"I don't mind the rain."

"All right then." He hesitates before facing forward. "Is this Jack Lord's compound?"

I pause, caught off guard. "Yes."

He squints at me curiously, but that's it. The taxi turns onto the main road, and I'm pretty sure we pass Maya and Adrian in a Mini Cooper. I twist around in my seat. They turn down the road that leads to Belmont's estate.

I huff as I face forward. I can't believe they haven't hopped on a flight back to the west coast. There's nothing left for us to say to each other. At least I'm not there. They'll probably see my car parked out front and knock, ring the doorbell, and shout my name to no avail. And after they give up, then and only then will they ship out. This is what I'm hoping.

"So you're a writer?" the cab driver asks as I sit stewing.

"Yes, I am," I say enthusiastically. It's time to get back on track. "Hey, if I give you a call when I finish the walk, will you be able to pick me up?"

"Yeah, sure." He pauses. "Are you friends with Jack?"

"Um, yes," I mumble.

He nods as if he's pleased. "He's a good guy."

I'm about to agree when we pass a wedding caravan featuring a horse and buggy parade. I watch the bride being wheeled in the lead cart while the rest of the wedding party trails behind her. The women wear satin, pastel dresses and the groomsmen are in gray pinstriped suits.

"Could you slow down?" I ask as we pass. I fumble my camera out of the bag, switch it on, and click away.

"I heard there are thirty-nine weddings today. There were fifty-seven yesterday and seventy-five on Saturday," my driver says.

"Is that so?" I take shots of the horses, the bride, and the wedding party. It's strange how subdued they are. Maybe because it's still early.

"It's wedding season," he says.

"Sorry, I didn't get your name?"

"I'm Todd."

"And you live here on the island?"

"Ten years."

"Where are you originally from?" I'm done taking pictures, so I turn around and the car speeds up.

"Rhode Island. Providence. Where are you from?"

"California. Los Angeles."

He nods. "I can see it."

I chuckle. "I get that a lot."

"You've got a look about you. All the sun and surf and dentists…"

"Ah, the white teeth." I laugh. "That's a recent phenomenon. Hardly anyone smokes in L.A. anymore. And there's all the granola."

"Granola?"

I grin. "Non-acidic foods don't stain the teeth."

He narrows his eyes at me through the rearview mirror as if that's a bit too much. "So what's your story about?"

"Um, it's part of a taxicab series. Although I'm thinking I should abandon the theme."

"Is that why you called me?" He sounds excited.

"Yes." I smile. I'm glad he's enthusiastic about the idea.

"You want to use me in your article?"

"That'd be nice."

His blue eyes study me again through the rearview mirror. I can see his thoughts churning. Todd's a decent-looking guy. He's young, maybe in his mid- to early twenties, and has fine blond hair and very pale skin. "I would take you up on that if I were a crook. The worst way to see the island is by cab. It can cost you."

"I'm starting to figure that out." I sigh, nearly yielding to defeat. Martha's Vineyard doesn't have that grungy taxicab feel.

There's no fifty-mile ride to a small village where I can find a local spoon, a boutique hotel for the night, and a couple of locals willing to tell me how to avoid a brush with danger in order to find a hidden jewel like a majestic waterfall, or secret beach, or pristine valley. Then two days later, when I'm done with that little town, I call the same taxi driver, start up a brand-new conversation, and have him drop me off at another location that's also off the beaten path. That can go on for weeks. The longest I've ever toured by cab-driver guidance was three months straight.

Martha's Vineyard will probably only take two days, three days tops to get through this entire island. And why pay an extra three hundred a night to stay in a hotel that's only twenty minutes away from Belmont's estate?

"Well here's the bridge." He pulls off the road and into a turnout. "Take the bridge into the foliage, and there you go." He digs a business card out of his pocket. "You can call me when you're done."

"Okay," I say as I dig my wallet out of the bag. "How much do I owe you?"

"Don't worry about it."

I flinch, taken aback. "But you said…"

"No worries." He waves off the forty dollars I try to shove at him anyway.

"Okay," I say as if struck by illumination. "Should I pay you at the end of my trips?"

"Whatever."

I sigh. I certainly don't want to force money on someone who doesn't want it. I'll respect his wishes and pay him later. I slide out of the cab to walk the damp trail. It's cooler out this way. It might be sixty degrees.

I walk on automatic pilot. The trees are short and stout. They may be white oak and beech. I'm snapping away at the beauty, and the farther I walk, the deeper into the forest I go. I can smell sassafras–nice. The green foliage, hovering low to the ground, the tree trunks twisting like they're dancing, the mystery of not knowing what's around the corner all make this walk feel like a suspenseful scene in a novel. All I can hear are birds chirping and my camera clicking.

When I glance down at the wet trail, I remember yesterday and Belmont taking me to the ground in a moment of passion. Having him here with me would be nice. I wouldn't get any work done, but he's pleasing company.

He's a gigolo, a voice whispers in my head, attempting to taint my feelings for him.

I sit on a stone bench under a canopy of trees. A few seconds later, a group of people pass. We smile at each other. Another group passes. Then there are more and more. They're not all dressed up, but I take it that they're heading to the same place. Curiosity makes me follow them past a meadow of wild flowers until we're out of the woods. I gaze out at the waves that roll onto shore from the horizon. It's a breathtaking sight—the fishing village to my left and the cliffs to my right. In the center, a wedding is about to take place.

Then it dawns on me—this should be my angle.

Wedding Island...

Nuptial'ville...

Wedding Crasher...

That's what I'll do! I'll write an article on all the different weddings on Martha's Vineyard. With fifty or so a day, it shouldn't be difficult. Fueled by my new purpose, I head back to the road to summon the cab. I hadn't realized how far I've come.

Once I reach the road, I call Todd, and he's quickly on the way.

As soon as I slide into the backseat, I announce, "I'm crashing weddings."

"Like the movie..." he comments, grinning.

"Yes. I plan to blend in and take pictures. I wish I could get a list of all the weddings taking place this week."

"I can get you that," Todd says. "I've got a friend who works for the recreational licensing department. You need a license for every damn thing here on the island."

"Really?" I nearly shout. "You can do that for me?"

"Yeah. Why not? You're nice, and I like you."

"Yes! Yes! Yes! Please!" I'm so excited that I clutch his shoulder and shake him a little.

He laughs, delighted he could make someone so happy. "I'll make a phone call. I'll see if I can get it for you today."

He does just that. I'm sitting on the edge of my seat as he speaks to his friend. At first, the friend seems hesitant. When Todd mentions that I'm staying at Jack Lord's compound, there's a long pause. He says "yeah" a few times. Then he hangs up.

"Two hours," he announces.

"Thanks!" I sing in celebration.

Since I'm hungry, he takes me down-island into Oak Bluffs to have lunch at Linda Jeans, a diner on Circuit Avenue. I ask him to drop me off on Oak Bluffs Avenue, and I'll walk to the diner. Since I have two hours to kill, I want to tour the popular street and take some pictures.

"Be back in two or less," Todd assures me before he drives off.

Once he's off, I realize that I still haven't paid him. I'm sure my bill is close to a hundred bucks, if not more.

Circuit Avenue is an average, quaint little tourist trap. I don't find tourists traps at all repulsive. Au contraire! They have been built for our amusement, and isn't that what vacationing is all about? I click pictures of T-shirt shops, the candy store and the ice cream parlor. I take the stairs into the one and only coffee shop on the street since it's about time I got my latte fix.

I enter and before I take the first step toward the counter, to my surprise, I see Charlie in a booth with a girl who looks to be a teenager! She could not be his hot, heavy phone call from earlier. I think my shock shows because he hops up out of the booth and comes over to me.

"What are you doing here?" he whispers near my ear.

"Getting coffee. What are you doing here?" I glance at the girl. Goodness, she's young.

"I'm with a friend."

"How old is she?" I whisper, hoping she couldn't hear me over the crazy rock instrumental from the seventies playing.

"I don't know—legal," he replies.

I snicker at how stupid that answer is. "Charlie, she's really young. How old are you?"

"The same age as you."

"I'm thirty-five."

"Get the hell out of here!" he nearly shouts.

"Yes. Are you thirty-five?"

"I'm twenty-seven. I thought you were younger."

"What?" I grin cynically. "You thought I was jailbait like her."

"She's not jailbait, Daisy."

"She's not twenty-one, and if she told you she was older than that, then she's lying." I don't know why I'm going at him so hard. I mean, why do I even care? If her parents don't burn him at the stake, then why should I? "Never mind." I wave a hand passively. "Have fun."

"Wait." He takes my arm before I can take one step. "I'd still rather, you know, be with you."

"Not an option," I quickly say.

"I know. I'm merely stating a fact."

"You better hope that girl is at least eighteen," I say after taking another look at her. She's scowling at us. Then I realize Charlie has a hand on my waist. "Later, Charlie." I kiss him on the cheek and go order my vanilla, non-fat latte.

Charlie returns to the booth, says something to the girl, and they get up together and walk out the door.

That was weird.

I take my latte across the street to Linda Jeans for lunch. I sit in a booth across from the bar and order a tuna sandwich and garden salad. I take out my pad and jot down some notes as I go through my shots, recording the sights, smells, touches, and tastes of my walk.

I get distracted when I hear a man at the bar say, "Jack." I wonder if he's referring to "my" Jack. I should probably call Belmont to tell him I'm very close to forgetting last night's ordeal. My major organs miss him—my heart and brain. My skin craves his touch.

"He's got a full crew in Gay Head," one of the men says.

They're both wearing dusty denim pants and work boots.

"He'll put you on. Don't worry about it," the other one replies.

"What's going up in Gay Head?"

"Some hippy commune."

The other guy laughs. "How long?"

"I don't know. They keep changing the plans. They're all involved—the reservation, conservationists, and city hall. Troy's pulling his hair out."

The guy who's looking to get put on a crew snorts.

One of them, the one with the shaggy haircut but clean-shaven face, looks at me. He grins. Jeez, I've been staring without even realizing it. He lifts a hand, and I'm forced to exchange the gesture. I put my eyes back on my work. As soon as I do, the waitress sets my order in front of me.

"Thanks," I tell her.

"You're welcome," she replies.

I keep my eyes down to eat, however I continue listening to the men talk about Jack and his job sites. Apparently some men on the crew just returned from Haiti. They were working for him there, too.

"He's got work almost everywhere," the one guy says.

Their conversation turns to how the Patriots are faring, and that's when I stop listening. I'm up to ten pages of notes when Todd sits down across from me and drops a thick packet next to my plate.

"Here you go, Daisy!"

"Thanks!" I beam as I open the large orange envelope and slide out a small stack of papers listing the details of the weddings occurring on the island.

"She said that list goes out until the 15th of December."

"Nice…" I study the data. "How much do I owe you for all of this? I mean, put it all on the bill. The ride to Menemsha, the ride here, the wait—"

"It's nothing. Just doing a favor for a new friend."

I squint suspiciously. If he lets me off the hook without paying a dollar, then that will certainly be a first. "What's going on?"

"Nothing. It's free. You don't like free?" He smiles. "This is the Vineyard. We're giving here."

I open my wallet even though I smell Belmont's interference. "Well, if there's anything I can ever do for you, don't hesitate to ask." I give him my card.

That reminds me of when Belmont gave me his gray business card. I still don't understand what's stopping me from making that first move. Maybe it's the list. I'm too excited about my story and wedding crashing with my camera to be distracted. If I call him now, then he'll want to bed me, and I'll want him to bed me.

"You got it," Todd says. "You still need a ride, don't you?"

"Oh!" I say and lift a hand to claim the waitress's attention.

We head back to Jack's house after I pay the bill.

CHAPTER 10

It Ends With A Kiss

There's a sticky note on the door that has, "We'll talk when you're home," written in Maya's handwriting. Wow, is she overconfident. I snatch it off the wood, crumple it up, and throw it in the kitchen trash can.

It'll actually be good to get out tonight to see if they're any hotspots to write about, but I'm still obsessing over the bathtub upstairs. Every girl has her vice, and mine is a scrumptious bath. Before I program myself another hot bubble bath, I email Dusty Burrows and pitch my new idea to him while telling him why Martha's Vineyard isn't suited for the taxicab series. I have a message from my mom, but I'll open it later. She's probably just checking in; she does that once in a blue moon.

I notice some changes as I stand between the bedroom and bathroom. The bed has been made, the sink and tub have been scrubbed, and a lemony-fresh scent lingers. Belmont's housekeepers must've come while I was out.

I hurry over to the vanity and pick up my cell phone to ask him to join me, but then I reconsider. I still don't have the extra time to be sidetracked by Belmont Lord. I'll wait until tomorrow to apologize for my overreaction and tell him that, beyond reason and without a doubt, I love him. Tomorrow has to be dedicated to crashing weddings and taking enough photos and gathering enough details to send something a little more solid to Dusty. If Dusty refuses to accept my new angle, then I'll pitch it elsewhere. Decision made, I strip out of my jeans, T-shirt, and underwear and ease into the tub.

I could choose to read The New York Times or listen to Billie Holiday, but instead I close my eyes and think about how naked I am. I still don't understand why Belmont is so turned on by me. I've never gotten the general fascination men have with a woman's anatomy. They're just breasts and butts and arms and legs and whatever else they find so tanta-lizing. Men have the same body parts, for goodness sakes! I can't deny how he makes me feel–desired, needed, and more beautiful than I thought I could ever be. Finally, I feel like a woman.

Memories transport me back to yesterday. The ocean water was cold, but our mouths were delicious and warm as we kissed against the jagged rock. As I relive that moment and simper, the doorbell chimes.

My eyes pop open and my heart pounds. Who in the world could that be? It can't be Belmont or Charlie because neither of them is big on ringing or knocking. According to

Maya's Post-it, she and Adrian have shipped out. Although she could be staging a fake-out, but I think she's gone.

Maybe it is Belmont. Instead of coming right in, he's allowing me to make first contact by unlocking the door and inviting him in. Am I ready to sacrifice my plans for tomorrow to make love to him tonight?

Absolutely!

I stand so fast my head turns dizzy. The doorbell chimes again.

"Coming!" I shout even though there's no way he can hear me from up here. My skin is still wet when I wrap my red kimono robe around me. It clings uncomfortably to my wet skin. It won't be on long anyway. I hear the pitter, patter of my damp feet as I run down the hallway. Since my feet are wet, I carefully descend the stairs.

Once I make it to the door, just to make sure it's him, I look through the peephole.

I gasp and step back.

Maybe this isn't happening.

Maybe I'm still upstairs in the bathtub and I've fallen asleep. I pinch my arm.

"Mom, is that you?" I ask cautiously.

"Yes, it's me."

I anxiously turn the two bolt-locks and swing open the door. "Mom?" I'm still stunned. "What are you doing here?"

"One of your friends told me you were here."

"Maya?" I ask, thinking maybe she was telling the truth after all when she said she spoke to my mom.

"No. Belmont Lord. He flew me in."

I'm speechless. I still can't believe I'm looking at Heloise Krantz in the flesh. I haven't seen her since Easter. She has the same long, bone-straight salt-and-pepper hair and the flawless skin of a teenager. My mom is fifty-five, but she's always taken for a woman who's in her early thirties. She's a mixture of French, Spanish, and English, while my dad is Senegalese and Creole. They're probably the reason why I've been infected by the traveling bug. I'm a product of the world.

"Daisy?" she gently asks. "Are you going to let me in?"

"Oh yes," I reply spastically and step back. "Why would Belmont call you?" I close the door behind her.

"He said you weren't in a good place. He filled me in."

"On everything?" I ask.

"Everything," she confirms. "Daisy, why didn't you call me yourself?"

I roll my eyes as if the answer is obvious. "Mom?"

"Why do you say, Mom?" she replies snippily in her barely there French accent.

We're getting off on the same foot as usual. "Just… Nothing." I shake my head, mindful that I'm behaving like a moody teenager.

For the first time ever, I take a moment to look into my mom's light green eyes. She's not at ease because I've put her on guard. Is that the effect I have on her?

"I apologize," I say. "That was rude of me. Truly, Mom"— my voice cracks—"I'm really happy to see you."

She opens her arms. I accept the gesture and go in for the hug. My mom always smells like gardenias. She's two inches taller than me, and I always liked that. Her height made her extra powerful in my eyes. I used to warn the kids in grade school that my mom could beat up their mom. She is an Amazon-gladiator–feminine, yet strong.

"I can make us coffee," I say, still in her embrace.

"I will make it," she replies and kisses me on both cheeks. "You are still ma fleur, Daisy."

I smile, realizing that I haven't heard her say that to me in years. I run her bag up to the room I slept in last night. I wouldn't dare usher my mother into a smaller bedroom than mine. When I enter the kitchen, she's already found a coffeemaker, coffee, and filters and is measuring out the grains.

"Go sit," she instructs as she moves around the kitchen, opening and taking things out of the cabinets and refrigerator.

I follow her command and sit at the end of a long table set in front of a big dark window. As soon as the coffee's done she serves me a hot cup of it. I sip the brew and watch as she whips up salmon and egg scrambles and a kale salad with pomegranate seeds, sliced apples, pears, and oranges.

"I see you cook now," I remark.

She sets the chef-styled plate in front of me and then sits down beside me with her own plate. "I had to learn someday."

I take a bite of eggs. "Um, this is good, Mom!" I'm pleasantly surprised.

"The truth is I take a cooking class on Sunday mornings to help with the stress."

"I thought you mastered the art of living happily with stress."

"Me too, until I fainted in a meeting."

I freeze with a forkful of salad near my lips. "You fainted? Did you go to the doctor?"

"Yes, I did, and she told me I was stressed. I told her, that's nothing new. She told me, neither is death."

I try to picture what my life would be like without my mom in the world. Suddenly I feel the loss in my heart. I clear my throat. "Are the classes working?"

She smiles a little, sensing that I'm choked up. "They are, ma fleur," she assures me. "So… let's talk about the man with the private airplane?" She's purposefully changing the subject.

"Belmont." I simper and look bashfully into my coffee cup.

When I lift my eyes, my mother is regarding me shrewdly. "You like him?" she asks.

I nod. "I kind of do."

"He is rich," she concludes with lifted eyebrows. "But is he on the up and up?"

"He is," I assure her, although I wonder what made her ask that question.

"And you know this?"

"I think I do," I mutter indecisively. After I think about it, I amend my statement. "No, I know he's good."

She calmly takes another sip of coffee. I sort of feel like she's the Don and I'm asking her permission to be in love with someone.

"Hollywood is small, Daisy." She lifts her eyebrows as if she's hinting at something.

"Is it?" I'm confused.

"It is. And I once met a man named Jack," she hints.

I expel a long sigh of dread. "You know, don't you?"

"And he knows that I know," she replies.

"And?" I wait on pins and needles.

She shrugs in dramatic fashion, slowly and elegantly raising one shoulder with a slight twist. "Who cares, Daisy? I didn't think you would."

"I don't. Not anymore."

"Then that is good," she sings optimistically. "Jack Lord was a beautiful boy with a fool's dream. He was smart enough to get the hell out of the shark's tank so that he could make something out of himself."

"But did you and him..." I've stopped breathing, waiting to hear the verdict.

"Absolutely not," she replies. "Now"—she shimmies her back against the suede high-back chair—"tell me everything."

And that's exactly what I do. I start with my dinner with Adrian three months ago and work my way up to this moment. Before I know it, three hours have passed. We've cleaned our plates and switched from coffee to burgundy that's so fine even my mom approves.

"Why haven't we ever done this before?" I ask after my second glass of the red.

"Because you chose to stay away."

"But you never want me around." I sigh, feeling sorry for myself.

"You are so wrong, ma fleur," my mother says as she squeezes my hand. Her fingers are nimble and soft. She withdraws her hand and downs half a glass of wine. "I don't get an award for Mother of the Year. Not from you, Elita, or Iva"—she sighs and pauses as a veil of sadness covers her eyes—"or Daniel."

I flinch, surprised to hear her say that. I feel so bad about her self-criticism that I say, "You were fine, Mom."

She snickers first and then studies me for a short while. "It is easier, isn't it?"

"What do you mean?"

"To speak the lie. You tell me what you think I want to hear, and then you're miserable and I'm happy. You get that from your father, Jacques. Daisy, ma fleur, I did not want to be a mother. Ever. I love all of you because you are mine, but I liked you more when you could wipe your own ass and come and go as you please. Only, by then, I'd screwed it all up. You're not much different from your sisters. If anything, you can help them. You survived me. They're not doing so well."

Dear God, my mother is tipsy. She slouches in the chair and closes her eyes. "Fuck them. That pansy you called a boyfriend and that cock-sucking whore you called a friend." She opens one eye to study me. "Did you know she offered to blow my Joseph?"

"What? No!" I'm more shocked to hear that than I am to hear Heloise speak to me as if she's one of my fouler-mouthed girlfriends. Joseph is my stepfather, an executive producer and creator of three hit network dramas.

"You brought that filthy tramp to my anniversary party, and she cornered him and offered him a blowjob in exchange for an audition."

"Oh, I'm so sorry, Mom," I say sincerely.

She snorts. "Oh, don't be." She pats my shoulder. "Joseph informed her that I have an exclusive contract with him in all matters of fucking and blowing."

I let out a loud, unrestrained laugh. That was the funniest thing I've ever heard. Strangely, I can picture my mom doing it. She's that attractive. I once asked her why she doesn't color her hair. I'm thirty-five and inherited the gray gene. I color my hair twice a month every month. She said she would color her hair when she gets enough wrinkles. She'd paid her dues and taken her lashes, and the gray is a reminder of that. Each strand says, "Don't fuck with me because I've been around a long time."

Heloise Blanchard—Heloise Krantz after divorcing my father and marrying Joseph Krantz—worked her way up from a gofer to President of Pygmy Park Studios. She resigned to head a smaller operation where she produces my stepfather's hit shows. Needless to say, they do pretty well for themselves.

"And Andrew…" she continues.

"You mean Adrian?" She never gets his name right.

"Whatever." She flips her hand dismissively. "He calls your father too much"—she also calls Joseph my father—"kissing his ass by giving us reports on you. The only reason I don't tell him to go straight to hell is because you never call or stop by. If you were dead, I wouldn't know."

I feel like shrinking into my chair. I didn't know Mom felt that way. But I don't apologize because she's right; I should say what I think and not what will make her feel better.

"I didn't think you cared. After Daniel died, you and Dad checked out. I thought without him, you didn't want me."

She reaches over and strokes my hair. I'm stiff. I can't believe I said that, but it's the nucleus of everything that's wrong with our relationship.

"We were going to divorce before Daniel died," she finally says. "I could be nothing but a shitty mother and Jacques could be nothing but a shitty father. We did the best we could. I'm always doing the best I can, ma fleur.

"You and Daniel were easy. You had each other, and Jacques and I, we retreated like cowards. The first time I knew we had it too easy as parents is when you were four and Daniel was six. It was a Saturday afternoon, and I was taking calls and panicking over deliverables. Finally, I remembered I had two little children. I said, 'Fuck, I haven't fed them all day!'

"But when I found the both of you, you were in the back-yard building a dog house." She chuckles at the memory. "Daniel dug all the tools out of the garage and then dragged you door to door to ask the neighbors for any spare wood they had lying around. You also made peanut butter and jelly sandwiches–lots of them."

I've never seen my mom smile like that. It's refreshing. "I don't remember that."

"You were too young. And there are too many similar memories buried on top of it."

"Like the tree house debacle." Now I'm wearing the same smile, remembering my brother, my hero. "And the fifth dog house debacle."

"He also tried to dig a second swimming pool in the front lawn. Five times. Build a house for only you and him to live in. Screw us…" She chuckles. "That's what he said. He was mad at me for forgetting your birthday."

I lift a finger. "I remember that."

"You both used to get your skateboards, and we wouldn't see you until dinner." She narrows her eyes inquisitively. "Where did you go?"

"To the park to jump the benches. Once we skateboarded all the way to Hollywood Boulevard and Long Beach." I pause. "And Malibu and Santa Monica. We tried Pasadena, but I wimped out at the 10 Freeway."

"Is that so?" Mom asks, half impressed, half amazed. "I would've never let you do that if I knew."

I shrug and joke, "Well, you were too busy being a shitty mother."

She laughs in the way one does when they've had too much to drink. "I hope you let me make it up to you."

I kiss her on the cheek. "You've already started. But, Mom, if you didn't want children, then why did you marry Joseph and have two more?"

She sighs, getting cozier with the chair cushions. "Because he wanted them. You know these goddamn people; they have their ideals. He's a good father though. Thank God for that." She falls silent, and I study her beautiful face as she becomes more and more human to me. "Listen, ma fleur, when you get home, call Jacques. Go see him and say to him what you said to me. He would like to hear it." My eyes grow wide, and she catches it. "You're not coming home?"

"Yeah," I say, but I don't sound convincing.

"Is it that serious between you and Jack Lord?"

I shrug and mutter, "Maybe."

"And you met him on Saturday?" Her tone is colored by doubt.

I nod continuously, grinning. "Yeah."

She studies me with narrowed eyes. "Humph."

"What is it, Mom?"

"I never thought you'd fall in love with anyone other than Daniel." She massages my shoulder. "It's quick, but hell, I believe it. I knew this is how it would have to happen for you. Joseph and I used to talk it about it all the time. We knew you didn't love Andy—"

"Adrian," I quickly correct her.

"Andy, Andrew, Adrian, who cares? I'm glad I don't have to take any more of his phone calls. But we knew it would have to sneak up on you."

"What would have to sneak up on me?"

"True love."

"Oh…"

"This is good. I'm happy for you." She smiles at me and strokes my cheek. "Ma belle fleur."

Our conversation turns, and we talk about everything under the sun. She wants to know about my job—where I've been and where I'm going. She vents about all the imbeciles she has to deal with on a daily basis, including tomorrow. She has to fly out first thing in the morning.

"First I let them take my accent, next they'll take my life," she complains.

But I accused her of loving every second of it, and she had to agree.

We fall asleep on the sofa in the enclosed patio, watching the ocean and finishing off the bottle of wine. At five o'clock in the morning, the alarm on Mom's cell phone rings.

Mom darts upstairs to shower and brush her teeth. When she comes back downstairs, she's wearing a tight pair of boot-cut jeans and a sheer, button-down white blouse with a silk camisole under it. She emigrated from France to California when she was ten years old and never looked back. My mother puts the California in California girl.

I offer to drive her to the airport, but she insists on taking a taxi.

"Get some real sleep, Daisy. You have a man to make up with today," she says and hugs me good-bye.

She's now gone. And I can't wait to properly thank Belmont Lord for bringing her to me.

$$\wp$$

I take my mom's suggestion and set the alarm on my phone for ten a.m. before climbing into bed. When the alarm sounds, it's loud and imposing. I groan as I climb out from under the sheets. I had four glasses of burgundy too many. If it weren't for my aching head, I would doubt that my mother was actually here last night. We've never spoken to each other like that. Ever.

That's because I had an epiphany recently. Leaving things the way they are is merely my way of maintaining emotional and spatial distance. So much of my life has been lived already, but in the last three days, I realized I want more. I simply want more.

According to the list, the first wedding was scheduled for nine a.m. this morning at Blue Meadow Ranch in Chilmark. According to the map, the estate is only six miles away from where I am. I hate that I missed it. I mark the next six weddings and two receptions I plan to crash. The brides and grooms are all from big cities like Baltimore, Manhattan, Chicago, and Alexandria, Virginia. I should be able to fit in easily.

According to the forecast, today's high will reach sixty-eight degrees. That's pretty nice for this side of the country. I decide to wear a dreamy, powder-blue cashmere wrap-dress and gold two-inch high heels. I've already accepted the fact that by the end of the day, my feet will be throbbing, burning, and stinging. Only another warm bubble bath, this time accompanied by Belmont Lord, will sooth them. I know I should call him to thank him for what he's done for my mother and me, but the pressure of six weddings in ten hours is weighing down on me.

I straighten my hair with the flatiron and twist it into a chignon at the back of my head, allowing loose strands to fall around my face. By ten thirty a.m., I'm behind the wheel of the rental car and plugging all the addresses into the navigator. Three of them are at farms, two are at lighthouses, and one takes place in a meadow. One reception is in the courtyard of the Ocean View Inn in Edgartown and the other in Vineyard Haven.

The Martha's Vineyard landscape is becoming familiar to me. My senses have gotten used to the oak, birch, maple, cedar, and sassafras trees. I expect to be swamped by trees at every turn, but there's a surprise around every corner. You're driving or walking along and then out of nowhere, a meadow of wildflowers opens up or a shimmering pond where ducks play appears. And I can tell how gentle a place is by the varieties of fowl that live there. Wild geese flap through the sky, safe and secure, knowing that there are no hunting seasons on Martha's Vineyard.

The first three weddings go just as planned. I take pictures. I always choose the bride's side because her guests are the most talkative ones. I make comments to strangers about how beautiful the flowers are, how fantastic it is that the day has finally come, and embellish by saying "I saw her already, and she's stunning." That's how I usually get the name of the bride.

"Yeah, Tabatha picked the right dress this time."

"Leanne deserves this moment."

"I'm so happy Rachel decided to go through with it."

"Hell, it cost her enough... Sidney is always big on spending big..."

Of course I can't use these tidbits in the article, but I become part of the guest list just as if I received my own invitation with the big day announced in gold lettering.

I'm in the meadow at wedding number four and have been going at it nonstop. Sidney's chipper friends Carly and Linda have taken a liking to me. The attendees are from Chicago, and we've already discussed ad nauseam the sheer number of men who live on the island while waiting for the tardy bride to step on her mark.

"Dirty hands, dirty mouths... plain old dirty," Linda remarks in a plain old dirty way.

"I know I've seen you somewhere," Carly says for the fifth time as she squints at me. "How do you know Sidney?"

And now I'm forced to confess. "I don't know her."

"Then you're friends with Emil?"

I shake my head. "No. I'm a travel writer, and I'm writing a story about weddings on Martha's Vineyard."

Carly snaps her finger. "That's it! You write that taxicab series! I mean, the photos of you leaning on the taxicab alone make you want to read the articles. I'm like, 'I want to go wherever she's going.'" She laughs.

"What taxicab series?" Linda asks, still confused.

Before I'm able to say a word, Carly explains my work. "And Sidney is a bigger fan of your articles than I am! She would die if she knew you were here, at her wedding. Wait, I'll be back." She shoots out of her seat and trots up the aisle.

The next time I see her, she's standing in the aisle waving for me to follow her. Everyone looks concerned as she takes my hand and nearly drags me along. It does appear as if something has gone terribly wrong.

But au contraire—I hit the jackpot!

Sidney, the bride, gives me permission to snap as many photos as I like. She says she would really like to have an editorial-quality shot of the moment they turn to face the audience after being pronounced man and wife. On top of that, she'll grant me an interview tomorrow morning before they ship out for their honeymoon on the French Riviera. They chose that location after reading my article and plan to follow my excursion step by step.

I also lucked out that she's a stunning bride. Her figure, face, and dress are very editorial. Sidney is tall, curvaceously fit, and she has wavy brunette tresses streaking down her back. Her dress is white—that's classic—and I'm so happy she's wearing a vintage pearl necklace.

The groom is an ordinary tall, thin, shaved guy. He makes me wonder, How in the world did he land her? This, of course, makes the article even more appealing. They represent the promise. If you have your wedding on Martha's Vineyard, even if you're an average Joe, you just might end up with a Sidney. There's no way Dusty Burrows will turn down the article once I send the shots.

I'm in writer mode, paying attention to all the little details. I snap a shot of the little girl with ginger ringlets at the moment she's handed the satin pillow with the ring by a smiling bridesmaid; the awestruck expression on the groom's face the moment the bride appears; two women whispering about how breathtaking she looks; how her father's face turns from dutiful to pleased the moment he hands her to the new leading man in her life. I certainly get the money shot that Sidney requested. The birds in the trees, the sky with its bulbous clouds, and the yellow wild flowers are also featured in nearly every shot.

After the ceremony, Linda and Carly insist that I attend the reception. They promise there will be a horrible wedding band belting out all of the hits from the eighties and nineties, but no one will care how bad they sound because they'll be wasted as soon as the party starts.

I'm not a big social drinker, so I decline until I'm offered a spot at the dinner table—I can't refuse food. I hadn't realized it, but it's going on six o'clock and I haven't eaten at all. This happens frequently when I'm working. Only when I'm on the verge of fainting do I remember it's time to eat.

The wedding party proceeds from the meadow to the docks where a number of boats wait to whisk them across the shores to a mansion in Edgartown that once belonged to a sea captain.

I head back to the car to call Belmont and let him know where I'm going. I search my wallet for the card he gave me, but I can't find it. And he's never called my phone, so I don't have his number.

I chuckle at this minor disaster. I make a split-second decision to drive to his house and knock on the door, but there's no answer.

This time, fate isn't on our side. I retrieve my notepad from my bag, rip out a sheet of paper, and write out a note telling Belmont that I've gone to a wedding reception in Edgartown. I leave the address. It's actually kind of disappointing that he isn't at home.

The drive to the reception is a solemn one, and I can't help but speculate about where he might be. Maybe he was called away on business. Maybe I was right and I was a game he played. But then why would he go through the trouble of flying my mom here? Apparently they had a serious conversation. Nope, he's serious about me. He truly cares about me— me, Daisy Blanchard.

That puts a smile back on my face as I navigate the dark roads. Daylight Saving Time is no more and I already miss it. I roll into Edgartown and find a parking space just large enough to accommodate one Mini Cooper.

This street brings back bad memories. Boy, did I overreact the other night. Instead of escaping, I should've remained at the table, kissed Belmont proudly, and replied, "So what? Now are we done here?" Thus, wiping that smug look off Maya's face. If only life granted do-overs after cooler heads prevail.

I snap photos while advancing up the street. There's nothing more enchanting than Main Street of a small town in autumn. Almost all the quaint storefronts have white lights strung in the windows, and the glass-house streetlamps add to the ambiance. Usually the sidewalks are made of red brick, and the one street separating them is so narrow that I could hop right across it in two leaps.

On a scale from one to ten, the pain in my feet has reached seven and a half. I'm sort of limping with each step and alter my plans for the night. I won't stay for dinner. I'll take photos, thank the bride for her generosity, and confirm our interview for seven a.m. at the Day Harbor Café where we'll have a light breakfast.

Finally, my aching feet bring me to the lawn of the mansion. What a novel idea. Blocks of white lights carve out a pathway leading to the white canvas tent. With the lights twinkling in the bulbous shrubs and feathery trees and the mansion rising in the distance, one would think that they've just stepped into the pages of a fairy tale.

The closer I get, the more chatter I hear. The guests erupt in laughter. A woman is speaking into a microphone. It's too early for a toast, but that's what it sounds like. Aching feet and all, I pick up the pace to capture the moment.

"Kiss, kiss, kiss, kiss…" the crowd chants.

"Ah, what the hell!" the woman says.

I make it just in time to catch the kiss, camera in hand. My mouth is caught open. I'm frozen behind a table of people cheering on the kissers.

To my utter shock, it's Belmont and a sultry brunette, and they're engaged in some serious tongue action. My fingers involuntarily snap the shot as I take steps backward. Before I know it, I'm running away from the tent, across the lawn and down the street.

Heck, I can't win for losing!

I snatch the car door open, forgetting to turn off the alarm first, and it starts blasting. After fumbling with the keys, I'm able to silence it. Once I close myself inside, I preview the photo.

His hand is on her waist. Their lips are locked. My heart once again shatters. I can't take this any more. Instead of pain, I feel numb and resolved to the fact that every decision I've made regarding my love life has been a bad one.

I close my eyes to settle my breathing. Maybe I had to meet Belmont in order to make things right with my mom. And maybe he can't help himself. He was, or is, a man whore. He's a nice guy, well meaning, but maybe his sexual cravings are unquenchable. Since I left him wanting, he found another woman to fulfill them.

There… that's how I make sense out of what I just saw. I sift through my contacts and call Leslie, my travel agent. I wait with bated breath for her to answer.

"Charter One Travel, Leslie speaking," she says.

I expel a sigh of relief. "Hi, Leslie, this is Daisy Blanchard…"

"I know who you are!" she says excitedly. "How are you doing, sweetie?"

The fact that she speaks to me as though we're not the same age doesn't bother me this time. Instead, I go right into spouting out instructions.

"I need you to find me a house to rent that's not in Chilmark or owned by a Belmont or Jack Lord. Please tell the owner that he or she is not to divulge my whereabouts to anyone; as a matter of fact, don't even provide my name. Make sure there's a wireless Internet connection. I need the rental until Saturday morning, and book me a flight out of Logan to Lima, Peru that afternoon. Oh, and make sure it's a refundable ticket. I might fly back to LAX instead." I've decided to accept the Peru offer, but I'm also itching to have that conversation with my father.

"What's wrong, sweetie?" she asks, concerned by my dry, unemotional tone.

"I'm sorry, Leslie, I didn't even say hi."

"That's okay, but are you okay?"

"I'll feel better if you could secure a house for me within the hour. Don't worry about the expense. I'll pay it."

"Of course I can," she claims in her usual overconfident manner. "I'll call you shortly with the details."

I tell her thank you before she hangs up.

I'm on automatic pilot but still numb as I drive back to Belmont's house. I rush inside and dash upstairs to pack everything. I want to cry but refuse to. I go to the office and pack up my computer. I search the cabinets until I find paper bags to take the food that I bought. I make six trips to my car and, as a result, work up a sweat.

My cell phone chimes as I stand in the doorway with my suitcase in one hand and computer bag hanging on the opposite shoulder. Leslie's name is on the screen.

"Hello!" I exclaim hopefully.

"Get ready, sweetie, here's the address…"

It's official. I'm leaving. Suddenly, I can no longer hold back the tears, and they pour out of my eyes without much effort.

CHAPTER 11

Looking For Her

❦

Belmont Lord

*B*elmont Lord thought he saw a familiar face out of his peripheral vision. He tried to do a double take, but Mandy Hill had yanked him by the collar to slather him with a wet kiss. She tasted like vodka and a breath mint. His tongue went numb, which meant that, along with being drunk, she was high. He wanted to be anywhere but there.

Suddenly he had what felt like an out-of-body experience. He was watching himself kissing her and wondering when in the hell she was going to stop. Everybody was egging them on. A sick feeling rose up in the pit of his stomach, and he felt as though he was making a monumental mistake.

Her tongue dug deep in his mouth, threatening to stab his tonsils. He had to put a hand on her chest and shove her back as gently as possible. Dinner hadn't been served yet, and most everyone was already wasted–including the bride, the groom—who was a friend of his—the best man, all the groomsmen, bridesmaids, and even the goddamn parents.

"Finally!" Mandy slurred, shooting her arms up victoriously. "I've been wanting to do that since college!" She fell down on her knees and announced that she wasn't going to blow him, at least not yet, but she asked him to marry her. Then, in a shocking move, she tried to unzip his pants.

Belmont had had enough. He wasn't in a joking mood, and he was the only one who wasn't laughing. He was going on two days and nights of no sleep. He'd been sure Daisy would've called him by now. He understood why she was angry. What had happened the other night was not only all bad, it was all wrong. And to think, he'd been the one insisting on meeting up with that certifiable skank and Daisy's ex-boyfriend, who was not at all who he expected. He was scraggy and whiny, the type of man who didn't deserve someone like her.

Thinking about how much he missed Daisy made his bad mood worse. He'd lost track of her this morning. He knew Todd had picked her up yesterday and taken her to Menemsha. He picked her up again and took her to Oak Bluffs. After that, Todd dropped off the radar because he had to fly out to Manhattan on business.

Belmont raised a hand to the drunken guests and scurried down the platform stairs. He almost returned to his seat, but then he remembered he was sitting next to Mandy. That was how he ended up standing there beside her in the first place. So instead of taking his chair, Belmont dug his cell phone out of his pocket and pretended to receive a call. It was a pathetic move, but he already had enough and now it was time to leave. He kept walking until he reached the Beamer, got in, and drove home.

He rode past the turn that would've taken him to Daisy. He really wanted to hold on to the hope that she would contact him and do it soon. He'd already broken his word—once on the trail—but he just had to have her. Belmont couldn't put a finger on it, but touching, smelling, and tasting her, being inside of her felt like the joy of getting his first dirt bike for Christmas when he was nine years old.

He loved that she was unpredictable. Not in a crazy-chick way, but in the way where she kept her emotions close to her. When she chose to reveal them, it was like a well-played hand of cards. He also loved the fact that she was a travel writer who'd been just about everywhere and did so alone. He loved that she was beautiful, definitely knew it, but couldn't truly give a damn. He loved that she loved water, like showers and the ocean. Geraldine, the maid, reported that she'd taken a bath twice. He loved her spirit and her energy and how being near her made him feel whole again.

Belmont felt a lump in his chest as he turned down the driveway to the house he was staying in. "Goddamn it, Daisy," he muttered. She was killing him, and he didn't know how much longer he could hold out.

He decided to leave his car parked along the motor court just in case Daisy called during the night. He didn't want to have to open and close the garage before jetting out to get to her.

As soon Belmont let himself inside the house, he needed two aspirin and a tall glass of water. He plodded into the kitchen, and he was caught off guard by the unholy sight of a naked girl rummaging through the refrigerator.

"Excuse me," he asked carefully, sort of ticked off at Charlie for keeping her on a loose leash. What if Daisy had been with him?

"Hi," she sang and giggled, giving him a full frontal show. She was trying to appeal to him by pushing her hip to one side and lifting her chest high. "You're Jack Lord, aren't you?"

"And you're in my refrigerator," he grumbled.

"Oh well, I was hungry." She pushed her hip out to the other side. "Munchies." She giggled.

"Well, did you find what you were looking for?" He regretted the question as soon as he said it.

"Now I have," she crooned, fondling her tits.

Belmont watched her for a few seconds. He couldn't deny that he was repulsed. Her age had a lot to do with it, but the fact that she wasn't Daisy was the biggest reason. He wanted to see Daisy standing right there, stark naked and playing with herself. He'd pay a million bucks to see that. He'd probably fuck her into the deep freezer. That thought worked on him, and the little girl, whoever's daughter she was, had to either go back to Chuck's bedroom or go home.

"Chuck!" Belmont shouted over his shoulder. "You left something in the kitchen!"

The girl suddenly stopped playing with herself and looked petrified. In a short while, Charlie strolled into the kitchen—butt naked—shoved his tongue down the nervous girl's throat, and slapped her bare behind.

"Go get your ass in bed," he commanded.

"But I didn't get anything to eat," she whined.

"Oh by the way, Daisy stopped by," Charlie said.

Belmont could not believe what he just heard. "What? When?" he asked spastically.

"About an hour ago."

"What did she say?"

"I didn't talk to her because I was occupied, but she left that."

Belmont's eyes followed where Charlie's chin pointed. He stomped over to the edge of the kitchen counter and retrieved the paper. He read it until he got to the part that made him sick to his stomach.

"Fuck!" he shouted. "Fuck! She was fucking there?"

"She was where?" Charlie asked, confused by Belmont's outburst. He'd never heard Belmont say "fuck" three times in a row.

"She was at the wedding. She saw it!"

"Saw what?"

"Mandy kissed me."

"Ha!" Charlie laughed, amused by his brother's unfortunate situation.

Belmont had no time to glare at him. He spun on his heels, swiped his car keys off the counter, and ran out the door. He had a lot of explaining to do.

Once again Belmont felt like his life was playing out in slow motion. He couldn't wait until all of the shitty drama passed. He vowed to never leave making the first move up to Daisy again. Her timing was way off, and she took way too long to come around.

He drove double the speed limit, and he almost lost control of the vehicle and veered into the woods. Thankfully, the car recovered quickly. He wouldn't let an accident get between him and Daisy's body.

She was at the wedding. He knew he'd felt her near. Belmont never believed in soul mates until the moment she walked past him and he almost lost it. She was wearing dark shades, but he knew she'd noticed him for one second. Then she noticed Kara and dismissed him. He watched her continue up the dock with the sad realization that to her, he was out of sight and out of mind.

He'd figured Martha's Vineyard was small enough to find her, and he would go looking for her. That night, he fell accidentally in bed with Kara. They had too much to drink and both needed to lie down. She started playing with his pole, and the next thing he knew, it was inside of her. He couldn't stay up, so he faked it. He didn't know why he couldn't go all the way. He didn't have a girlfriend, but he was in love—in love at first sight with a woman he'd never met. It was crazy and stupid as hell, but he couldn't help it.

In the morning, he'd sat down with Kara and explained that he was wrong for having sex with her. Of course, she didn't see it the same way. She thought—deep down inside—she loved him.

Belmont hated hurting women. Women in pain had comprised his client list when he worked as a male escort—husbands or boyfriends were cheating on them, husbands paid them no attention, or they were going through a messy divorce or breakup. He learned enough about the opposite sex to know that it was best to bite the bullet and tell the truth.

That way Kara would get over him and find the person who would treat her better than he ever could.

How ecstatic he had been to be rewarded for his honesty. He left the house to give Kara time to gather herself and leave, and he went to the Day Harbor Café for breakfast. Belmont sat inside to be alone and sulk, and that's when he saw Daisy sit down at a table on the patio. He watched her for a while. That sensation in his head returned and his endorphins stirred. She wouldn't get away from him that time.

In front of the house Daisy was staying in, he jumped out of his car, slammed the door, and ran up the steps. The lights were off, so he figured Daisy was asleep. He would surprise her, wake her with a kiss, and keep her up all night long. He wouldn't be able to get enough of her until his body zonked out on its own.

Belmont unlocked the front door and walked upstairs. He was shocked to see the bed made. He felt sick in the pit of his stomach. He stomped over to the closet. Her clothes were gone. Her suitcase was gone. He searched all four bedrooms, the office, and the kitchen. There was no sign of Daisy anywhere.

He lost the strength in his legs and bent over to clutch his knees. He wondered if she could've left. Maybe she went to the wedding, saw the kiss, and then hopped on either the eight thirty p.m. or nine thirty p.m. ferry to Woods Hole.

Belmont had to think. Daisy had to return the rental car first. The office stayed open until eight p.m. It was Tuesday. Adam worked the Tuesday-night shift.

Belmont recovered enough to place the call, and Adam reported that she hadn't returned the car yet. That was a relief—at least that was something. He chose not to waste another second. Daisy would be found come hell or high water. She had to know that what she saw at the reception was not what she thought.

Belmont jumped into his car and sped off. He started with all of the inns in Chilmark. He searched the parking lots and went inside to ask if Daisy had checked in. Next he did the same in Aquinnah, in Edgartown, then Menemsha. He was worn out by the time he arrived in Oak Bluffs and had almost fallen asleep at the wheel twice. But he would not give up. He pressed on to Vineyard Haven. He was able to get a cup of coffee at the Rest Ridge Inn; Daisy wasn't there either. Two hours later, four o'clock in the morning, he had finished his sweep of West and North Tisbury.

At least he'd accomplished something. He let everyone know that if she happened to walk through their door, then they should call him. Adam promised to leave word with every shift to call him as soon as Daisy returned the car.

By the time Belmont made it home, the sun was rising, and he could barely keep his eyes open. He knew he'd find her soon to clear up the misunderstanding. Charlie was still in his room with the girl, who was screaming and making crazy noises. Belmont didn't have enough energy to bang on the door and shout something like "cool it." As soon as Belmont's head hit the pillow, he was out.

CHAPTER 12

The Morning After

There goes my alarm.

As soon as I wake up, my feet feel as if they've gone nine rounds with Mike Tyson only to get knocked out cold, and so does my head and my entire body. I groan and drag myself over to the dresser to stop the buzzing.

I'm renting the guesthouse of one Thelma Clary. My guess is that she's part hippy and part crazy bird lady—although maybe they're one and the same. Last night, she'd assured me that I would remain safely tucked away. She added that she knows how it feels when a girl needs to escape. She mentioned that she knows every single bozo on the island but wouldn't push me for a name, although she's sure she knew him. Before leaving me alone with my misery, she reassured me that I would not be discovered by the person I'm running away from and informed me that she'll have breakfast on the deck at seven a.m. sharp. I told her I would be meeting an interviewee in Edgartown at that time, but I'll join her from Thursday until Saturday. She seemed satisfied with that answer.

I kind of hoped Belmont would show up at the Day Harbor Café. I hoped he would sense that I'm here, at six forty-five a.m., sipping coffee and waiting for Sidney. Of course, I'll understand if she skips our little meeting. It is the day after her wedding, and the only reason she's still on-island is because the last ferry left before the reception was over.

Since I'm early and it's chilly outside, I sit inside. Only two people are here: the waitress who served me on Saturday and myself. She's very nice and surprised that I'm here at this hour. I ask her why.

"Tourists never show up this early."

"Oh. It wouldn't be vacation if you wake up before eight to eat breakfast."

She chuckles. "No, it wouldn't."

"Well, I'm going to be interviewing a brand-new bride shortly. That's my reason for rising and shining before the cock crows."

"Is that so?" she says, suddenly intrigued. "Why are you interviewing her?"

"I'm a travel writer. I'm writing an article on destination weddings."

"Oh how exciting!" She widens her eyes as if that's the best thing she's going to hear all day.

"Yes, the wedding was beautiful," I mutter. I'm already exhausted, recalling the reception and Belmont kissing his date.

"Morning, Daisy!" Sidney croons as she barges inside. She's glowing like a lamp, clearly happier than I'll probably ever be. She's keeping the bride theme alive by wearing a white maxi dress that outlines her luxurious curves.

"Good morning, Sidney." I feign a smile.

"What happened to you after the wedding? You never showed up at the reception."

"Oh." I sigh and try to think fast. "I had an emergency, um, back home."

"Oh..." She sounds genuinely concerned. "I hope everything is better."

"As well as can be." The sides of my mouth turn down as I break eye contact to take my notepad and recorder out of my satchel. "Do you mind if I record this interview?" I keep my eyes on the device, ready to press the "ON" button if she grants permission.

"Sure," she says, still a little concerned.

I look up and say with a lot more enthusiasm, "So why did you choose to have your wedding here on Martha's Vineyard?"

Sidney hesitates. I can see that my change in demeanor has taken her by surprise, but she seems to understand I don't want to talk about last night's circumstances, especially with a bride that I just met yesterday. "Well, when I was younger, we lived in Hyannis, and we had a house here on the island too. Just about every weekend, especially after the chaotic summer—have you ever been here during the summer?" She waits for my answer.

"No, I haven't."

"The island suddenly gets very small and cramped all the way from Gay Head to Vineyard Haven. My dad always wanted to avoid the crowds, so we spent more time at our vacation home during the fall and spring. We were always here on the weekends during the wedding season. I was so fascinated by the wedding processions and always knew that when my time came, I wanted to do it right here on Martha's Vineyard."

"You mean get married?" I wish I hadn't asked with such sarcasm—that was definitely a mistake.

"Well, yeah, Daisy, all little girls want to be married to their Prince Charming. Didn't you?"

I shrug. "It doesn't matter what I wanted. I'm interviewing you." I wink.

"Oh come on, Daisy! We're girlfriends now! Hell, I invited you to my reception!" She laughs.

I chuckle a little, although I'm wondering if I should tell her a lie or the truth. As an interviewer, sharing my thoughts and feelings can taint the interviewee's responses to where suddenly I'm getting disingenuous information and losing the vitality of the story.

"No, I really want to know. Wait. First, are you married?" she asks.

"No, I'm not."

"Do you want to get married?"

I shrug.

"What is this?" She exaggerates a shrug. "I'm not one of those women, you know, the marriage Nazis concerned about the next woman's fertility and ring finger. If you don't want to be married, then that's fine with me. Although I'm curious how someone who looks like you could stay single."

I chuckle. The last question I can answer easily. "That's because men do not marry for looks. Women believe that, but it's not true."

"You better believe Emil married me for my looks!" she exclaims jollily. We both laugh. "So tell me, Daisy the travel writer," she says on a more serious note, "why don't you want to get hitched?"

"You just assume that I don't?"

"I know that you don't because if you did, you would've said it already."

"Okay, then why did you get married?" I ask, forgetting the dynamics of the interviewer and interviewee.

"Because..." She sighs dreamily while gazing off. "Okay..." She drops her elbows on the table to get cozier. "You know how when you're having sex with someone you truly love and you can't get close enough to them? You want to merge into their soul, but it's physically impossible." She pauses to wait for any sort of response from me.

"Yes, I know that feeling." My reply is clinical, but my heart is pounding. From that first kiss in the car outside of the florist's house, I felt that with Belmont, and it's so awful because whatever emotion or power that was refuses to leave me.

"When I stood before the minister and made a vow to Emil, that's what it felt like."

I can't speak because I'm choked up. I swallow the lump in my throat. "That makes sense." I clear my throat and drive onward. "So… When you think back to yesterday twenty years from now, what will you remember most?"

Sidney's eyes dance as she recalls the big day. She nods continuously. "The boat ride… It was an enthralling disaster!" She goes on to explain how they got splattered with water and that she almost fell into the ocean twice. She turned back to get a look at her bridesmaids, and they were miserable. "But I would definitely do it all over again even if the idea was better than the actual experience!"

All in all, it's a good interview. After an hour, we exchange phone numbers in the contemporary way. I give her my number, she plugs it into her phone and then calls me right there on the spot and now I have hers. All that's left for me to do is save it to my contacts, which we both do at the same time.

Once she's gone, I order an egg white country-styled omelet, put on my headphones, and start transcribing the interview. Jeez, no wonder Sidney was so concerned at the onset of our interview. I sounded miserable; I probably looked it, too. Regardless, I trek through. Some parts make me smile and some make me laugh.

All in all, I'm very happy about what I have so far. I need more experiences and more interviews. I'm glad the list Todd gave me includes email addresses. Later today, I'll send an email to the brides to request an over-the-telephone or in-person interview.

Once I'm done eating, I take care of the bill and drive to the first wedding on my schedule. Keeping busy is the only way I'll be able to get through this day without breaking down and crying my eyes out.

The first wedding is in Vineyard Haven, and the couple is from Los Angeles. To my surprise, I know a number of the attendees and am able to acquire tons of information about the bride and groom. I receive a tip that I could undoubtedly land an interview with Jeritha Hope, the bride, by mentioning my mother, Heloise Krantz.

The next wedding is in Edgartown, and the final one is near the Campground in Oak Bluffs. It's difficult being here without Belmont. As I stand on the church lawn, waiting for the bride and groom to saunter out into the daylight, I gaze at the mint-colored gingerbread house that Belmont brought me to. It still looks unoccupied. I use my camera's high-powered lens to see inside of the upstairs glass doors. The checkerboard is still set. I catch a breath just as the crowd erupts in cheers. I don't have time to sulk and tear up. I turn my camera to the doorway of the church and capture the happy moment.

By two p.m., I'm done crashing weddings and fitting in by commenting on how beautiful "she" looks and how much "she" deserves this. My cheeks hurt from fake smiling and portraying bliss even though I feel like crap.

The beautiful morning has given way to a breezy, cool afternoon. I head back to North Tisbury. Thelma is outside planting flower boxes in front of the main house when I roll up. She waves at me, and I wave back as I drive past her.

Thelma really is a nice lady. I assume she lives here alone. She appears to be in her mid-to-late sixties. She reminds me of Katharine Hepburn in On Golden Pond with the same messy chignon at the back of her head and button-down shirt over a turtleneck.

I stop in front of the garage attached to the modest guest-house, get out to lift the door, drive inside, and close it. There's something refreshing about doing it the old-fashioned way. Walking up the sidewalk and watching the ocean roll onto the shore in the distance is nice. Once inside, I get right to work.

Dusty has replied to my email. He wants to see any preliminary information I may have before making a decision. I send him fifty of the best photos, displaying the diversity of each ceremony. I need more photos of the receptions, but I make do with the five I have from Sidney's, which includes that kiss between Belmont and the brunette.

I also write up a teaser, and a little inspiration allows me to write the first half of the article. It's more about travel than weddings. It's about the walk through the forests before arriving at the farmhouse or cliff. It's about getting married in a neighborhood of gingerbread houses or in an open meadow with the ducks playing in the pond in the background. It's about capturing smiles and little girls twirling in pretty dresses because they're bored out of their minds and would rather be swinging from a jungle gym.

The doorbell buzzes as soon as I hit send. I check the time on my computer; it's four p.m. I get up to answer the door.

"Hi, Thelma," I say with a smile. I would call her Ms. Clary, but last night she insisted that I call her Thelma.

"I have sandwiches and tea on the terrace if you're hungry."

Actually, I'm starving. The egg white omelet has run its course. "Sure! Let me just finish up here and I'll be right over," I say, thumbing over my shoulder.

"All right then." She seems both surprised and pleased by my response. Maybe she took me for some sort of recluse, which I am not. The truth is, I love meeting new people. I can't wait to hear all about Thelma, and I have a feeling she won't mind telling me.

By the time I reach my computer, Dusty Burrows has already responded.

> Daisy,
> I want this story. 2k words + 100 photos. $6,000 + travel expenses ($2,000 cap).
> DB

> I write back.

> DB,
> $7,000 + travel expenses ($3,500 cap) + 100 photos, then deal.
> Thanks.
> Daisy

> I stand back and wait. Not even a minute goes by.

> Deal.
> DB

I do a happy dance. That's a pretty good payment for a story that's not part of the taxicab series, which commands payments between $13,000 and $18,000 per article + 50% of travel expenses. Thanks to Belmont, my expenses will be far less than $3,500, but I asked for the extra cushion just in case.

Before I head out to the patio, I take off my dress and put on a pair of boyfriend jeans, a fitted, royal blue sweater, and flip-flops. The rest of the day will be leisurely because I'm high off of the sweet vibes of sealing the deal and knowing exactly what direction to take the article. I darn near float to the terrace.

"You certainly look pretty," Thelma says as I sit at the cast-iron dining table with a live fire-pit brewing in the middle. She's already seated, sipping on tea and reading the Vineyard Gazette.

"Thanks."

"Help yourself," she says.

My mouth waters as soon as I open the picnic basket. The fresh croissant sandwiches look delectable.

"Are you going to tell me your name yet, or what?" she asks with a coquettish grin.

I smile. "I'm Daisy Blanchard."

"And who are you hiding from, Daisy Blanchard?" she asks. It's funny because she hasn't taken her eyes off the newspaper. "Are you an actress or a singer?"

I chuckle a little. "Far from it." I bite into the sandwich. "Umm…"I close my eyes to chew. "This bread is so soft and sweet. I haven't eaten a croissant since Paris six months ago."

"I'm happy you like it."

"No, I love it."

"You sure you're not an actress? You're skinny and deprived of good food."

I laugh. "I'm deprived of food most of the time because I stay too busy."

"Then you're a workaholic?"

I lift my hand. "Hi, I'm Daisy Blanchard, and I'm a work-aholic." I grin.

Sitting here with Thelma, eating a turkey and cheese sandwich and watching the ocean, keeps angst from rearing its ugly head inside of me. It wants me to moan Belmont's name and cry over the kiss that I can't get out of my head.

She studies me with a smile. I think she's already guessed that I'm evading the initial question. "Whatever or whomever you're hiding from, sweetheart, I hope you find some peace while you're here."

"It's not like that," I confess, muttering.

"Then what is it like?"

Once again, I find myself starting from the beginning. The story of how I got here never makes sense if I don't disclose what Adrian and Maya did to me. "Then I met this man. He was perfect—at least that's what I thought." Only now does sadness color my tone.

"He's an islander?" she asks curiously.

I nod. "Kind of." That's all I'm willing to disclose about Belmont for now.

"Humph," she grunts thoughtfully. I can see her mind turning.

I'm hoping to death that she doesn't throw names at me. I will break down and cry if she asks, "Is it Jack Lord you're hiding from?"

"If you're not an actress and you're not in the witness protection program, then what do you do?"

"I'm a travel writer," I'm happy to confess.

"Have I ever read anything you wrote?"

"I don't know; have you?" I ask with a smile. "I usually publish nationally. I'm meeting with a publisher next month to discuss turning a popular series that I write into a book."

"If you're in the national publications, then I'm sure I have. What's your series about?"

"It's about how to use the distinct knowledge cabbies have to discover the hidden jewels you would've never thought to look for."

"What are you doing tomorrow night?" she asks, narrowing one eye curiously.

"I'll probably finish up some writing. It looks like it won't take as long as I thought it would, so I'll probably fly out on Friday."

"Well good, you'll be here. Every third Thursday evening, I have a big table dinner. Seven o'clock. Can you make it?"

"That sounds interesting. Sure."

"William Struggs will be there. He's the head of acquisitions at a major publishing house in New York. I think he would love to meet you."

"How are you, Aunt Thelma?" a man says as he walks onto the patio. He plants a quick kiss on her forehead and then his eyes gleam at me as he extends a hand in my direction. "Hi, I'm Pete."

I rise out of my seat to shake his hand. "Hi, Pete, I'm Daisy."

Pete is only a few inches taller than I am. He has dark brunette hair and thick eyebrows. He's not bad looking. As a matter of fact, he's quite appealing. If he had taken a seat across from me in an airport, I would have definitely done a double take. He looks like a manly man and is probably in his mid-to-late thirties. By habit, my eyes observe both of his hands. No wedding band. Either he's married and doesn't wear it or he's single. Not that I'm remotely interested, but finger checking is the automatic response when noticing an attractive man.

"Did I hear you mention the big table?" he asks Thelma while gazing at me.

"Yes, I did," she answers.

"And you're coming?" he asks me.

"Yes, I am," I say in the same casual tone Thelma used. I look at her, and she winks at me.

"Then I'll see you there." He finally lets go of my hand.

"Where are you off to?" Thelma asks him.

"I have a job further up the island," he replies.

Thelma explains, "Pete's an architect. He lives in Boston. He's here for work until Monday."

"Oh, nice," I say, attempting to sound as though I care.

Pete fishes a sandwich out of the basket. "See you tonight, Thelma. Hope to see you around, Daisy."

Once he's gone, I'm finally able to get the skinny on Thelma. She was married for forty-three years, but her husband died seven years ago. She used to be a painter but hasn't painted a thing since he passed away. She's originally from Charleston, South Carolina—which explains her slight southern accent—but she lived in Manhattan for thirty years before migrating to the island. After one visit to this piece of paradise, she and her husband decided to plant roots.

When I ask how she gets through a normal day—because I would be bored out of my mind if I lived here full time—she says she spends most of her time organizing fundraisers and setting up big table dinners. Apparently, the spots at her table are coveted by many. Suddenly I'm eager to see what it's all about.

"Do you like crab?" she asks out of the blue. "I think I'll make soft-shell crab for dinner tonight."

"I certainly do," I reply enthusiastically.

"Good, then that's what we'll have."

I grin. Sitting here shooting the breeze with Thelma is lovely. Suddenly, I don't want to push my flight up to Friday. "You know what? I think I'll stay until Saturday."

"You're welcome to stay as long as you like," she says.

I smile. "Thank you."

"Anytime," she says before heading to the kitchen to get dinner started.

I'm content, at least for the moment.

CHAPTER 13

Get A Clue

౸

Belmont Lord

The muffled sound of a cell phone ringing woke Belmont out of a deep sleep. He sat straight up and his eyes darted around the room. He searched for a way to turn off the chime. "What the hell?" Then he squinted down at his pants. The phone was in his pocket. He reached in and dug it out.

"Hello," he said, sounding jittery.

"Where the hell are you, Jack?" Troy, his manager at the Aquinnah work site, barked in his ear. "Andrea and I have been calling you all morning. The architect is waiting for you."

"Ah, shit," Belmont cursed and hopped out of bed. "What time is it?"

"Four-thirty. What the hell? Did you overdo it last night?"

"No," he sighed. "I've been having problems sleeping." He massaged his forehead. "I'm on my way. I'll be there in fifteen minutes."

He hung up and remembered why he was in such a state in the first place. "Daisy," he muttered.

He would have to continue his search for her after meeting with the architect. He was still in last night's party attire, but he had no time to change. He partnered with a non-profit to erect a private retreat. The goal was to build a structure that would coalesce with nature, which was why he'd asked Pete to design rooms that flowed into an atrium. It was an arduous undertaking, one Belmont almost passed on. The entire project felt too pretentious for his taste but he could use the tax break.

Belmont hopped into the pickup truck he used for work and zoomed up South Road. He used speed dial to call Adam. He had one question, and as soon as his friend answered, he asked it. "Did she leave yet?" Desperation flooded him.

"Nah, not yet, Jack. We'll call you when she returns the car," Adam reassured him.

Belmont felt more at ease as the truck rolled along the dirt road at the edge of the duck pond and onto the construction site. He planned to have Andrea, his assistant, get Leslie Birch, Daisy's travel agent, on the phone for him as soon as he was done consulting with Pete, the architect.

Most of the crew had left for the day, and the rest were just about ready to call it quits. As soon as Belmont exited the truck, he caught sight of Troy and Pete and took long strides in their direction. Although he'd been asleep for twelve hours or so, Belmont felt like crap.

"Jack, you made it," Pete said. "Rough night?"

"Sorry about that," Belmont replied. "Yeah, it was a long, rough night."

"You going to be okay, Jack?" Troy asked, definitely concerned about the state Belmont was in. He clearly didn't expect his boss to show up in last night's suit and looking like shit.

Belmont glanced at Troy, who was still watching him with ruffled eyebrows. "I'll be fine," he muttered. "So what do you think, Pete?"

"Troy was just telling me that they want to connect four open fields in the woods without harming any of the surrounding trees."

"That's right. It was a last-minute decision. All I need to know is whether or not it can be done."

"Let's see!" Pete sang enthusiastically.

Belmont lifted an eyebrow. He knew he had to be careful, ask the right questions, and rely heavily on his own experience when deciding whether or not the project could take such a dramatic turn. An architect was an artist, and Pete would take to the project like a hungry bear to a stack of honeycombs. So Belmont started the tour, guiding the two men down the natural trails the foundation wanted built into glass-walled hallways that would run between the structures.

An hour later, as expected, Pete was committed. He'd drafted some ideas as they went. The drawings had it all–tennis courts, gym, accommodations, dining facility, atrium, and a conservation park.

"We have to get the geologist out here first," Belmont said after studying the draft.

"Lowell's available tomorrow. If we don't catch him then, then we'll have to wait three more weeks," Troy chimed in.

"What time? Do you know?" Belmont asked, wearing a severe frown. His work was taking him further away from Daisy. If only he knew where she was. If only they were together without a doubt. Then, and then only, would he have a better response to having a reputable architect onboard and a solid plan to move forward.

"Five, six…" Troy said.

"In the morning?" Belmont complained.

"No, in the afternoon."

"Can't do it at six," Pete said immediately. "Aunt Thelma's big table dinner starts at seven."

"It's Thursday tomorrow?" Belmont suddenly remembered receiving the informal invitation.

He'd run into Thelma at the Menemsha Fish Market last Monday. She asked him about the work he was doing in Nicaragua and then invited him to her dinner on Thursday night. He had attended a number of them. It was equivalent to getting inside of the old boys' club. Over four hours or so of eating, drinking lots of liquor, and casual but stimulating conversation, a lot got done. Hollywood films were pitched; government policy made; and sometimes love matches were formed.

"Thelma has a guest. She's a travel writer," Pete said, revealing it as if he was bragging a little.

"A travel writer," Belmont strained to say. He felt the blood leave his face. He had no doubt that Pete was speaking about Daisy. Once again, fate worked in his favor.

Pete dropped his face, embarrassed. He mumbled, "Yes, but the point is, I have a dinner tomorrow evening. Five o'clock is my cut-off time?"

"Maybe Lowell can come out earlier," Belmont answered before Troy could. "I'll give you a call in the morning—bright and early."

Belmont planned to call all day long, up until dinnertime, just to make sure the architect kept his hands off of his travel writer. Plus, he had other plans, and as soon as he hopped back into the truck, he set off to fulfill them.

CHAPTER 14

A Slight Diversion

Just like the first morning I woke up on the island, I'm stirred by the chirping of a bird. It sounds as if it's perched right outside my window. This time, I jump out of bed to get a look. Upon seeing the little red furry bird, I gasp.

That cannot be the same bird we saw off the trail in the forest, the Scarlet Tanager—although stranger things have happened since I arrived. Its round and fuzzy chest is facing me, and its beady black eyes watch me. It must understand that we're separated by glass; that's why it's staying put.

This is the back of the house, the part that faces the thick forest. There's no way anyone will see me standing here wearing nothing but my white bikini panties, so I stand shamelessly, remembering how relaxing yesterday evening was. I was able to put my life in perspective over soft crab and two glasses of cabernet sauvignon.

Maybe I'm not meant to fall in love and all of that stuff. Every single relationship I had with the opposite sex has taken a turn for the worst. There's my real father, Jacques, who's a sourpuss in general. I'm closer to Joseph, my step-father—and that ain't saying much. My brother, who was more of a father to me than Jacques, died. Adrian, my first and only boyfriend... Well, he betrayed me in the worst way. Thank God, because his actions forced me to do what I should've done a long time ago, and that's admitting that I stayed because being with him was a facade. I could say I had a boyfriend, and that made me appear normal. I couldn't say that I had intimacy, or trust, or even a real friend in him, though.

If the relationship between Belmont and I had worked, that would have been nice. Then I could say that I had all three—intimacy, trust, and a friend. He, in the end, wasn't real, but at least I know now what my heart could experience if the real thing ever presented itself to me.

Suddenly my red, furry friend leaps off the branch and flies off like it's been disturbed. Its sudden flight takes me by surprise, and then I get the feeling that I'm being watched. My eyes seek and find the culprit. Pete is standing beneath the branches, boldly gazing up at me. It takes me a moment to remember that I'm topless. I take a step backward, and then another until I fall down onto the bed.

Jeez, Thelma's nephew saw my chee-chees! I wonder how long he's been standing there. Then I remember that I promised to have breakfast with Thelma at seven. There's no way I can bow out at this point. Was he being a Peeping Tom? It looked like he had on workout clothes. Maybe he was returning from an early-morning jog. There are trails throughout the forests. I'm sure that's it.

Feeling less embarrassed, I put on a green silk bra and a green striped sundress. I take a look at myself in the full-length mirror. Belmont accused me of always appearing sexy, and I certainly don't want that to be the case for breakfast. So I study myself at all angles. I don't think this dress could be sexy. It fits my body, but it's not tight. Pete will be able to see my green bra straps, but that's more of a fashion faux pas than anything. After another final pass, I conclude that I look fine–not sexy, but quite casual.

Just to be safe, I pull my too-straight hair into a ponytail. I haven't showered yet, but after breakfast, I'm going to wash the straight right out of my hair. Belmont was right; there is something sensual about the way my bushy, wavy locks sit on top of my head and spray down my shoulders. My current look is no frills or thrills. Maybe that will wash the sight of me standing in the window topless out of Pete's head–if he shows up for breakfast. Maybe he's just as embarrassed as I am.

So I slip on my flip-flops and head out to the deck for breakfast. I've never eaten as much as I have since yesterday afternoon. That's because Thelma keeps feeding me. I'm starting to become like Pavlov's dogs. She knocks to invite me over to eat and I'm instantly famished. My mouth is already watering imagining the next meal. As soon as I step outside, the smell of pancakes or waffles hits me. My stomach growls. It's ready to metabolize at least two stacks, which is a lot for me. Adrian used to accuse me of eating like a bird on purpose. At first it bugged me because that was definitely not the case. I simply only take what I need, even when it comes to food. I think it has to do with not overstepping my boundaries and remaining tolerable to others. However, when I work, I indulge—that's why I'm always on the road. I'm like Myrtle Wilson in The Great Gatsby. When I travel, I'm lively, extravagant, and oh so happy, like she is when she sneaks off to be with Tom Buchanan in the hip New York apartment. Everywhere else, I'm like her in George Wilson's garage: dull, miserable, and careful.

I nearly run back to the guesthouse when I see Pete is already sitting at the table. He's holding a Time magazine with one hand and sipping coffee out of a mug with the other. He's behaving as if he didn't see my breasts in the window.

"Good morning," I say, as chipper as possible, as I sit down across from him.

He lowers the magazine. Dang it! He's trying too hard to focus on my face. "Good morning, um…"

"Daisy," I remind him.

"Yes! Daisy," he says with a smile. "Now I'll never forget it."

"It's okay." I lift a hand as if to say no offense taken.

"Oh no…" He puts down the magazine. "I'm an imbecile for forgetting it. Especially since you're someone I would like to impress."

"Don't worry," I say as I scope out the spread. "I'm easily impressed." My nose did not betray me. There are pancakes, home fries, bacon, biscuits, and spinach quiche. Thelma has sliced up many different varieties of apples and pears. I pour myself a cup of coffee and add cream and a little sugar.

"I'm not easily impressed, but you've impressed me," he says hoarsely and then clears his throat.

I glance at him but only for a second. I debate whether or not I should come right out and ask him. I want to. Another thing Belmont has taught me is that it's okay to be direct.

"So, Pete," I start and wait for him to shift his eyes off of the magazine. "Did you see me in the window this morning?"

A huge grin spreads across his lips.

"I thought so," I say before he's able to say anything.

"I didn't mean to look. I was returning from a run, and there you were." He lifts his eyebrows as if he's entertained by the memory.

"I know," I say apologetically. "I should've thought better."

"Oh no," he quickly says. "Don't apologize. The pleasure was all mine." He's grinning.

I chuckle and drop my face bashfully.

"Why aren't you two eating?" Thelma asks as she walks out onto the terrace.

"We're waiting for you," he and I say at the same time. We both notice that.

"Well, here I am. Now eat," Thelma says. This morning, she's wearing a white linen dress with a navy blue cardigan.

"I like your dress, Thelma," I comment as I use tongs to retrieve two fluffy pancakes and a piece of spinach quiche.

"You're not so shabby yourself." She winks at me as she sits.

Right away she and Pete start talking about family matters. His father, her brother, is in the hospital. He has stage-three lung cancer.

She shakes her head. "I always warned him. I said, 'Peter, those cigarettes are going to be your demise.'"

"I know, Aunt Thelma," Pete says as if he's heard that a million times.

"Did you know he was a lobbyist for big tobacco?" she says, focusing on me.

I shake my head while chewing. "Uh-um."

"Both Petes are Republicans."

"Oh, come on, Thelma!" Pete groans like he's about to hear something else he's heard a million times before.

"My brother, I can see, but you, Pete, you're a stupid ass."

I do something that's between gasping, laughing, and choking.

Pete turns to me. As if he has to explain himself, he says, "I'm a Rockefeller Republican."

"Just like Rockefeller, they're all dead. You're going to have to come to the other side or adopt a whole new philosophy," Thelma says. "What are you, Daisy?"

"What do you mean?" I say after swallowing.

"What's your political affiliation? We're not coy at my table. You can speak without any backlash."

"Oh," I say and think really hard about the question. "I guess I'm nothing."

"Nothing!" she nearly shouts. "Whom did you vote for in the last election?"

My eyes bounce between her face and Pete's. They look as though they're waiting on the edge of their seats for an answer. Believe me, I know how people get about politics and religion. I've certainly found myself a witness to such debates but never a participant.

"I didn't," I'm almost afraid to admit.

Thelma studies me. "Why not?"

I shrug dismissively. "Because I don't buy it."

"What don't you buy?"

"I don't know—politics."

"Do you agree with Social Security?" she asks, and suddenly I feel like I'm being grilled.

I shrug again. "Yeah, I guess so."

"Medicare?"

"I guess—yes."

"What about funding schools?"

I nod. "Sure."

"What about a laissez-faire marketplace?" Pete asks before Thelma could throw a curve ball at me.

"Um," I hum, pondering while turning up my nose. "At what cost?"

"Ah-ha!" Thelma exclaims as she snaps. "You're a Democrat."

"Okay, well it must be politicians I don't buy into then," I say.

"Oh darling." Thelma pets the back of my hand. "You're going to be a lovely addition to the table tonight."

Pete chuckles and shakes his head. Suddenly, I'm worried. As much as I try, I can't believe the cream rises to the top when it comes to politicians.

As we eat, Thelma's questions never stop. Where am I from? Where did I go to school, meaning college? What are my parents like? Have I ever been married? Am I in love with whomever I'm hiding from? That's when I decide it's the perfect time to change the subject.

I shrug at her last question, dismissing it altogether, and say, "You used to be an artist. That's remarkable. I would love to see your work. I love art. I actually think I'm a connoisseur of great art."

"She used to run in Picasso's circle," Pete adds.

I throw him a thankful glance, and he replies with a smile. From that moment on, I learn that she did more than "run" in his circle. Some of her work is featured in Impressionist's collections in museums around the country.

"I feel an article coming on," I say, touching both my temples as if I've been struck by divine inspiration. "I know there must be dozens of artists like you, Thelma! I could feature you and a few other American artists who have hob- nobbed in the inner circles and track down your work in museums around the country. Heck, around the world!"

My eyes dance excitedly. I'm ready to forget about Peru and pitch this new travel piece to Life Art magazine.

"That would be lovely," Thelma says quietly—so quietly it kills my buzz.

"What?" I ask.

"I haven't painted since my husband died."

"Oh," I sigh. I should have remembered that. "I'm so sorry. I shouldn't have—"

"No, no," she cuts me off. "I love the idea. If you want to write it, then you have my support."

I haven't grinned this big since the last time Belmont and I made love. "I want to write it. I'm going to write it."

She squeezes my hand again. Thelma, Pete, and I smile at each other. For the next hour she gives me five names of other artists to feature, and she details living the life of an artist in Greenwich Village up until the late 1960s.

Pete's cell phone rang twice during our meal. Once, the person on the other end must've asked who's laughing because he answered, "Thelma's guest." They must've asked what did I, the houseguest, find so funny because Pete said, "Nothing. We're discussing the salaciousness of art." Then he stepped away from the table to find some privacy.

A little after ten thirty a.m., Thelma announces she has to leave because her quilting club meets at the top of the hour.

"What are you doing today?" she asks me as Pete and I help her clear the table.

"The ocean's calm. I'm going for a swim."

"Oh, I'll join you," Pete announces, boldly inviting himself.

I hide the fact that hearing that makes me shudder. I mean, he saw my breasts–both of them.

❧

Pete's cell phone rings again as we walk down the wooden steps in the cliff on our way to the beach. After he answers it, he shouts, "Now? I can't go now. I'm not going to go now."

"Go ahead," I whisper, waving. "I'll be fine."

He shakes his head emphatically. "I'm out swimming with a friend." After a long moment, he says, "Hello? Are you still there?" He pauses. "Okay." He presses the on-screen hang-up button and shuts the phone down. "There." He throws me a sexy smile.

I've seen that smile before. Actually, it's the way Javar Les used to look at me when he was teaching me how to swim—only I wasn't single then, and oh boy, did I let him know it. I'd called Adrian my fiancé, especially when Javar's underwater hard-on nudged me in the thigh or stabbed me in the butt. This time, I have no excuses.

Should I tell him that I could never be interested in him in that way? It's not that I don't find him attractive or nice or mildly interesting; it's just my heart can't withstand another disappointment. And it's still in love with the man I thought was my Prince Charming.

"I don't know what's going on with this guy," Pete mumbles while shaking his head.

"What guy?"

"I'm working for him. He's a piece of work."

"Oh," I say and let it drop. Obviously he doesn't want to elaborate.

"How good of a swimmer are you?" he asks cheerfully, changing the subject.

"Very good," I reply with confidence.

"A damn good swimmer or just a very good swimmer?" There he goes with that flirty smirk.

"A damn good one." Jeez, I'm returning the expression.

"So you can save my life if I drown because I'm a shitty swimmer?"

"Then you should stay near the shore."

We chuckle. We make it to the sand, and I catch him watching me as I take off my jeans.

"I have a swimsuit on," I mumble. He's leering as if he's going to see me in nothing at all.

"It's nice," he says. "Especially in the back." He curves his neck to check out my backside.

I snatch off my baggy T-shirt. "Pete, you're nice, but I'm healing"—I press my hand over my heart—"here."

"Sometimes the best cure can be a racy affair."

I refuse to look down at his junk. He's wearing tight swim trunks, and I don't want to know if it's swollen down there or not.

"Time to swim," I say and trot off toward the wonderful blue sea that's calling my name.

Pete is on my heels. He's persistent. He's obviously not going to give up until he gets what he wants. Javar Les still hasn't. He calls me at least twice every two months or so to ask when will I return to London or Paris. When I fly in to either city we always meet for lunch or dinner or a night on the town. And the visit always ends with him making moves that I subtly deflect.

Pete dives in right beside me. He matches me stroke for stroke.

"This way," he calls, and I follow him eastward.

We stay at it for a while, swimming along the shoreline. He's a good swimmer, way better than I can ever be.

"How's it going?" he asks as I start to run out of steam.

"I'm fine," I lie. "I'm just going to backstroke to dry land."

"All right," he says.

"You are an excellent swimmer," I admit while puffing. "I was trying to show you up, but you showed me."

Suddenly he wraps his arms around me. Dang it, even in the cool water he's worked himself up. Before I know it, we're kissing. My head isn't spinning. My heart isn't racing. All I can think about is how odd this feels. How wrong it feels. I pull away from him and backstroke toward the shore.

We're at least a quarter mile out when the current turns on us. My arms are heavy, and the muscles in my legs cramp. I'm definitely pushing it. The easiest way to do this is to flip over and free-style it to the sand.

Suddenly I feel myself being pulled under. I know I've been caught by a riptide. Usually I can swim my way out of one, but I'm confused and exhausted, unable to figure out which way is up and which way is down. I can no longer hold my breath and I choke. It doesn't take long to lose full control of my body and black out.

The next thing I know, I'm coughing and gagging water out of my throat. I'm on solid ground and freezing.

"Are you okay?" Pete asks, kneeling next to me. He sounds terrified.

"Yeah," I wheeze. "Now I am." Coughing and spitting up saltwater is not a pretty sight or a comfortable feeling. My throat burns and my head feels as though a vise is squeezing it.

"Better?" he asks as I quiet down.

"Better," I gasp and cough once.

Pete strokes my face like a good caretaker while staring into my eyes. "I have something to admit."

I frown curiously. I'm too weak to respond.

"I might have copped a feel and tongued you a little."

I laugh as much as I can, and my head turns dizzy.

"I think we should get you to the hospital," he says.

"No," I insist as I touch his shoulder.

"You really should get checked out just in case something's going on inside of you. I don't want you to fall asleep and choke on more saltwater," he says as he helps me to my feet.

Heck, that does sound scary. "Since you put it like that..."

Belmont Lord

"Pete!" Belmont shouted into the tiny device he crushed in his grip. The last thing Pete said was that he was going swimming with the houseguest. What the hell is happening? It's as if as soon as he takes one step forward, he stumbles ten steps backward.

Belmont was prepared to wait until tonight to see Daisy but he had changed his mind. He was in Boston picking up a special present for her. As soon as he landed on the Vineyard, he planned to drive straight to Thelma's and collect his woman. But at the moment he was stuck in traffic. In normal traffic, he would be at Boston Logan in fifteen minutes, but the mid-morning traffic was sure to delay him nearly thirty minutes. It would take another thirty-five minutes to land in Vineyard Haven. Pete had almost an hour to attempt to seduce Daisy.

The one thing Belmont loved about her most was what he feared. She's affable and always willing to go for the ride without knowing where she'll end up. Look how far Pete had gotten. Hearing her laughing that morning during breakfast was maddening. What in the hell did she find so goddamn funny? Did she miss him? It sure as hell didn't sound like it.

Belmont blasted the horn of the Porsche as if that would help. The car in front of him returned the gesture. When he finally made it to the airport garage where he paid to keep his car parked, he felt as if a thousand bricks had been lifted off his back. He grabbed his travel bag and hiked to the private terminal. He rushed through security screening and ran all the way to the jet. That drive actually took twenty minutes, and then they had to wait another twenty minutes to be cleared for takeoff.

The flight took another thirty minutes. As he sat, he wondered how he would find Daisy and Pete on the beach. Would they be lying beside each other sharing personal stories? Would she tell him all about her brother? Would she let him kiss her, touch her, and make love to her? Visualizing the progression made him crazy.

The small plane finally landed. Belmont grabbed his bag and disembarked in five minutes or less. He ran to his car, hopped into the Beamer, and raced to Thelma's place in North Tisbury. He parked in her driveway and ran to the back of the house to search out below the cliff. He looked across the sand and out in the water. Daisy was nowhere to be found.

"That was a short swim," he mumbled and then remembered why their swim was cut short. He did not want to discover Pete and Daisy together, but he would rather know sooner than later. What would he do if he discovered them having sex? He didn't know. He would probably beg her for answers. Why didn't she trust him enough to come to him about what she saw? Why would she think he would ever choose Mandy Hill over her?

Other than being a very fine actress, Mandy was a cokehead, which was why his tongue had turned numb when she kissed him. Of course he thought she was attractive in the manufactured, Hollywood way. Mandy reminded him of a real-life mannequin—too skinny and made of plastic. He'd known her for fifteen years, and since the first time they met, she'd made every major move on him in the book. He wished Mandy would teach Daisy a thing or two about being the aggressor. He'd always resisted Mandy because she tried too hard. There was also the cocaine, the partying—and he really didn't have any desire to smash skin and bones. He wouldn't even do her when she tried to pay for it.

He'd rather make love to Daisy's curvaceous and fit body. Making love to her made him feel like a fat kid in Willy Wonka's Chocolate Factory. Just thinking about it made his pants tight, and just picturing Pete drinking from his fountain infuriated him.

Belmont ran to the front door of the guesthouse. The sprint winded him, and he bent over to catch his breath as he knocked. After a number of seconds, he knocked harder. After that, he banged. "Daisy! Are you in there?"

No answer.

Belmont sighed, exasperated. He turned the doorknob. The door was unlocked, so he took the easy opportunity to look inside. The house smelled like her, and the scent ignited his taste buds. Shit, he had it bad. Self-preservation urged him to get out of there, but relief made him glad he entered and inspected the place. At least they weren't having sex there. Next Belmont rang Thelma's doorbell, but there was no answer.

"Damn, it's Thursday," he muttered. She was meeting with the quilt club at the Edgartown Library on the opposite side of the island. He checked his watch. Getting to the library would take fifteen minutes. Belmont sped all the way there. It took him only ten minutes.

The ladies were still inside when he arrived. As soon as he walked past the circulation desk and onto the main floor, they stopped sewing and chatting to focus on him.

"Thelma?" he said desperately.

"Jack?" Thelma definitely looked concerned about him.

Belmont thought to put on a smile. "How are you, Rosalie, Ana, Mable, Wendy?" He tried to remember his manners.

"Fine," each of the ladies replied. They also looked worried about him.

"Thelma, could we talk?"

"Why sure," she said. "Let's go to the reference room." He was all wound up as he followed her past the stacks and into a smaller space filled with larger, older books. She sat down in a blue, cushiony chair. "How can I help you, handsome?"

"It's Daisy," he replied as he sat beside her.

"Who's Daisy?" she asks, pretending to be ignorant.

"She's staying in your guesthouse. I love her." He figured he should come out and just say it.

Thelma sighed and dropped her poker face. "So you're the one she's hiding from?"

"She's hiding from me?" Being reminded that she was choosing to keep her distance kind of hurt.

"What did you do to her?"

"We had a misunderstanding."

"What kind of misunderstanding?"

"She saw me kiss someone else. Actually, she kissed me; I didn't kiss her."

Thelma shook her head. "You young people." After a moment of studying Belmont's lost expression, she patted his knee. "You want to come to dinner, don't you?"

"Yes. Exactly."

She sighed. "You know I'll always make a place for you. And Senator Howell will be there."

Belmont fought the urge to frown at the last part of what she said. He didn't know whether or not he was up to extreme networking. He had one goal in mind and meant to keep to it. "Thank you."

"You know Pete, my nephew? He's taken an interest in her," she said in a warning tone. "But she's too hung up on, I guess, you to take him seriously. I knew he didn't have a chance in hell." Thelma's smile turned smug. "That's why I didn't stop him. It's good for a man in his predicament to learn greener pastures aren't always his to graze on."

"Thank you," he said again as he rose to his feet.

"You're smiling, Jack," Thelma commented. "I guess the next wedding that pretty girl is going to be attending will be her own." She lifted her eyebrows, waiting for confirmation.

Instead, Belmont thanked her for the third time and strolled back to the car. Four more hours until dinnertime—that would be the longest wait of his life.

CHAPTER 15

Say Good-bye

"Do you smell that?" I ask Pete as we walk into the guesthouse.

"Smell what?" he asks.

I take in another whiff. "Forget it. I think it's the water in my head."

"The doctor said you were lucky that I saved you." He shows me that cunning grin again.

The doctor at the hospital checked my breathing, put me on oxygen for an hour, ran blood tests, and took a CT scan. He was quite thorough, to say the least. I'm sure I'll get the bill from my insurance company in the mail. I pay an arm and a leg each month, so it shouldn't be much.

"And I didn't know you could give mouth-to-mouth resuscitation while underwater. I was really impressed when I heard you did that."

"Again, my pleasure." We snicker. My head is a little too achy to laugh any harder. "I used to be a lifeguard while I was in college."

"Really?" I ask.

"Yeah, here on the Vineyard, during the summers."

We smile at each other.

"Well," I say, signaling that our time together has come to an end, "I need to get some rest if I'm going to make it to dinner tonight."

"Not before I make sure you're okay," he says and zips past me to the kitchen. "How about I make you a cup of tea and pour myself a drink?" He bangs around in there.

I sigh, deciding not to put up a fight. Heck, I don't want to be alone at the moment anyway–not yet. What happened to me is still a little frightening. I'm still trying to work up the courage to close my eyes and give in to sleep.

"I'm going to change into something more comfortable," I announce from the living room and walk upstairs to the bedroom.

I strip out of the T-shirt, jeans, and bathing suit, put on fresh underwear, and slide into a red lounge dress. I would rather go commando, but I don't want to send the wrong message to my company.

Pete is already relaxing on the sofa when I walk back downstairs. He whistles admiringly as soon as he sees me.

"Thanks," I mutter and sit in the chair across from him.

"So far away?" He's grinning salaciously.

I shake my head. "You never stop, do you?"

"Not until I get what I want."

209

"You already got it," I say as I lift the warm cup of tea off the coffee table. It's mint, one of my favorite flavors. "You tongued me twice, once while I was conscious even."

"I stole the kiss," he admits. "It was a good kiss. And"—he drops his face shamefully—"I did more than cop a feel. I had my hand on your tit the whole time. I didn't take it off until you came to." He shakes his head. "I'm terrible. Come on"—he waves his fingers toward his face—"hit me. I deserve it."

"How about we call it even," I say, keeping in line with our snazzy comebacks.

He chuckles a little. "Daisy, why are you single? You're perfect."

I sniff at the question I've been able to avoid for the last ten years. "I just got out of a long relationship, so I'm newly single. He left me for my best friend, so I'm not all that perfect."

"Oh." He flinches, taken aback. "Bummer."

"You're telling me." I take a sip of tea. I feel like I should say more since Adrian wasn't my be all, end all. "And then I met another guy, but he moved on rather quickly. He went from not being able to keep his hands off me to crickets. I saw him with another woman…" I pause. "Men suck." I relax against the cushion.

"You're right. We do. We really suck." He grins suggestively.

I snicker. "What about you? What's your story? You're a good-looking guy, and funny too I might add."

"Divorced, newly–sort of."

"Umm," I hum. I think I know this story well. "My parents are divorced too. Any children?"

"A daughter."

"Eek," I say like hearing that hurt. "That's tough."

"You're telling me. She's not taking it well."

"How old is she?"

"Eight."

I nod. "That's not a bad age for divorce. She probably won't remember how much it hurts ten years from now."

"From your kissable lips to God's ears."

I tsk lazily. My response is so weak that Pete decides to leave without being asked and allow me to rest. I ask him not to tell Thelma what happened today. I don't want her to worry. She might insist that I stay in bed, and I'm too curious about the big table dinner to miss it. He promises to comply but only for a kiss.

Since I've already done it once today, I do it again. Of course he embraces me and gives it to me good. Unlike Belmont, he doesn't have octopus hands. I want to put a million kisses between me and Belmont. Maybe I'll kiss some more boys while in Peru and then take a trip to London to finally give Javar that kiss he's so diligently pursued.

"Deal sealed," I whisper as I pull away.

Like Belmont, Pete's "Peter" has sprung to life. Lust is ablaze in his eyes. "You sure you don't want company?"

"I'm sure," I say as nicely as possible.

He swallows and then thumbs over his shoulder. "I'll be over there in case you change your mind."

I lock the door behind him, drag myself back upstairs, crawl under the blankets, and fall right to sleep. When my eyes open to a dark room, I'm aware that it's past seven p.m., and I'm late.

"Shoot," I curse under my breath and throw the covers off me. I rush into the shower and wet my hair just a little to seal in the waves. Tonight, I'll wear makeup and a little glossy-pink lipstick to match my soft pink, cashmere sweater dress. My shoes are black patent leather, high-heeled sandals with a shiny black patent leather daisy flower over the toes. Cute.

The night is chilly, but the door to the main house is only a hop, skip and jump away. Once inside, chatter touches my ears. One man is speaking louder than the rest. My heart pounds as I walk down a long hallway and then a short set of steps. I'm nervous and eager.

"May I help you, ma'am?" someone asks behind me. I turn and see a man in a formal white shirt and black pants.

"I'm here for dinner," I say.

"What's your name?"

"Daisy."

"And your last name?"

"Blanchard."

He smiles. "This way, Miss Blanchard." He leads me down a shorter hallway until we make a sharp turn into a sunroom facing the beach.

"Daisy Blanchard," the man announces.

All the conversation comes to an abrupt stop. I gasp in disbelief. Belmont Lord rises to his feet. Our eyes connect. Suddenly I feel like we're the only ones in the room. Then I see the girl he kissed at the wedding sitting beside him.

My eyes narrow without my prompting.

What a jackass.

He slowly takes his seat.

"Daisy, you made it!" The host sings jubilantly. Thelma's wearing a white, blousy, drawstring dress with tiny red flowers embroidered around the neckline. Her shoulder-length auburn hair is full of curls. She looks ten to fifteen years younger. "Daisy is a writer who doesn't vote," she announces to the group, beaming the entire time.

There's a collective, exaggerated gasp.

"There's one for you, Senator," a man—who has the timeless good looks of a retired tennis player—says.

Thelma curls an arm around my waist and leads me to the empty seat beside Pete. I avoid eye contact with Belmont, who's sitting directly across from me. I'm still shocked.

"And you're the travel writer?" the man on the other side of me asks.

"Um, yes," I say, blinking hard. I attempt to bring myself fully into the moment. Is this real? Am I having a nightmare?

"William Struggs," the middle-aged man who sort of looks like a modern-day Abraham Lincoln says. I shake his hand. "I read your work. We should talk more."

"Talk more about what?" I reply inelegantly.

"Publishing your articles."

"But I'm already in talks." My skin has run hot, and I can hardly concentrate. I can feel Belmont's eyes burning into my face.

"I'll give you another offer to entertain. It's best to have more than one suitor."

"Oh, yes," I say, distracted, as I finally allow my eyes to meet Belmont's. "Since you put it that way."

The table at large is still discussing the voting habits of people "my" age.

"What about you, Mandy? You're a young, beautiful movie star," says a man who's a cross between Colonel Sanders and the guy from those beer commercials featuring the most interesting man in the world.

All the eyes around the table dance to the woman, the actress, who kissed Belmont—all eyes except his.

"I don't give a fuck," she says with a dismissive flick of the wrist.

An elegant woman who reminds me of Morticia from The Addams Family says, "And this is why the country's gone to shit. Apathy." She flips her long black hair and shakes her head.

I think she's directing that nasty comment at me and the actress, but I don't think either of us takes it personally. Pete puts his hand on my thigh, and I think Belmont notices because he shifts uncomfortably in his seat.

"What about you, Daisy?" Belmont asks loudly. "Who would a wishy-washy person like you have voted for?"

"I'm not wishy-washy," I say defensively. "Politicians say what they have to say to get elected, just like men say what they need to say to get laid. Have you ever done that, Jack Lord?" I narrow my eyes at him. If he wants to go there, then I certainly can and will. He glares at me, and I cower under the power of his eyes and look down into my lap.

"Can we just vote for the one with the biggest dick?" Mandy says with her eyes pinned on Belmont, seeking to take his attention off of me.

The table erupts in laughter. Pete laughs too and cozies up to me, pressing his shoulder against mine.

"Are you two together?" Belmont blurts out harshly, shifting a finger between Pete and me. He's angry, and it shows.

Pete is trapped. He didn't see that coming.

I narrow my eyes at Belmont, warning him to stop. I'm embarrassed because all of Thelma's guests are watching us. "No," I finally reply.

"The question is, are you two involved," Morticia says, regarding Belmont and me.

"Then why are you letting him put his hand on your leg?" Belmont growls, ignoring the woman's comment. He's singled-minded at the moment.

"You mean like this?" Mandy squeezes him beneath the table before I can respond. Belmont tenses as his eyes expand. "Wow! Is that for her or me?"

Belmont grabs her hand and smashes it onto the table. "Stop it."

The moment is awkward. It's quiet, and Mandy frowns at me, blaming me for what he just did to her.

"Jack, the senator told me recently that he admired your clean water projects in West Africa and Central America," Thelma says in an effort to win back the table.

I've never seen him so angry. He's the one who kissed his date, and I'm thinking they've done much more since they showed up for dinner together. He's behaving as if he doesn't want her to touch him. I know they didn't live through two days without sex–that wouldn't be like the Belmont Lord I know.

"What about it?" he grumbles at Thelma while keeping his eyes trained on me.

"Jack?" she calls louder and snaps her fingers to get his attention. "Tootles, over here!"

He rips his eyes away from my face. Suddenly, I can breathe.

"Do you know Jack?" Pete whispers. I nod stiffly. "It's him? The guy you were talking about earlier?"

Again, I nod.

"Shit," he curses under his breath.

"What?" I'm eager to understand his reaction.

"I work for him."

"Oh…"

"What do you do?" Mandy asks Pete to both of our surprise. Her eyes flirt with him.

At first Pete hesitates, and then he mutters, "I'm an architect."

"Really?" She sounds genuinely interested and goes on about a house she just bought in Vail that she wants to renovate from top to bottom.

It's funny, but the more they talk, the more Pete leans into me. I'm not sure if he's a naturally touchy-feely person or it's his way of letting me know that he's still interested after learning that I was once involved with his boss.

Belmont is stuck in a conversation with a man seated near the head of the table beside Thelma.

Thelma smiles at me, and then she gets up and walks behind her guests to squat between me and the publisher. "Pete told me that you nearly drowned this afternoon?" As soon as I gasp over being betrayed, she smiles. "Don't be upset with him. He's powerless against me when it comes to keeping secrets. I've been his aunt for thirty-seven years." She winks. "Jack Lord stopped by the library today."

I glance at Belmont. He's saying something about purchasing equipment by way of fund matching. Actually, I want to hear what he's talking about. It's interesting. He's interesting. I'm impressed by the casual way he speaks about his remarkable work. He's not bragging or seeking acclaim. Actually, he looks like he really doesn't want to discuss it at the moment, which I'm sure he doesn't.

"I know all about the two of you. I hope you're fine with him being here," she says, but it sounds like she's asking me.

"It's fine," I mutter. "I just wish he wouldn't have brought her."

"Mandy Hill?" she whispers, surprised. "Don't you know who she is?"

I shake my head. "His wife?" I nearly gasp, hoping that's not the case. I mean, who else could she be?

"The Bloom is Off the Rose? Summer Lust? Tag Along Rider?" she asks as if those titles should ring a bell. I still shake my head. "You don't watch movies?"

"Not many. The last ones I watched were Lord of the Rings, and that was on DVD."

Thelma tilts her head back and lets out a delightful chuckle. "I'm too old to sit like this. Yoga can only take a body like mine so far." She finally stands. "Sweetheart, Jack Lord came here alone," are her last words before moving down the table to talk to another guest.

Right after she said that, Pete laughs at Mandy's comment, lifts his arm, and rests it on the top of my chair.

Belmont grinds to a halt mid-sentence. Suddenly, he shoots to his feet like an arrow. "Daisy, come." He stomps off as though he expects me to follow like a puppy in training.

Once again the table turns silent. My skin burns from embarrassment. They're watching and waiting to see what I'll do next. Keeping my face down, I scoot back my chair.

I look at no one as I tiptoe out of the sunroom and into the main house. Belmont stands right there in the tight foyer. He grabs my hand and pulls me along. I hear the guests erupting in laughter. There's no way I can return to that table after this.

However, he's touching me again, and we're so close to each other. I find that so satisfying. He leads me out the way I came in. I watch the effortless way he walks. He must be wearing part of a Tom Ford suit. I admire the way the pale gray, pinstriped pants shift with his sexy legs and the gray vest hugs him around the waist. He's wearing a crisp white shirt under it, rolled up at the sleeves. I hadn't noticed how stylishly he's dressed because I was trying like crazy to avoid his blazing stare. His outfit, of course, turns me on even more.

"Did you lock the door this time?" he asks as we approach the guesthouse.

"No," I answer. I wonder what he means by "this time." Earlier today, that familiar scent I smelled was his!

Belmont opens the door and tugs me into the house. Once we're inside, he holds me tightly, and his mouth attacks mine. He's kissing me hard; even if I wanted to stop him, I couldn't.

The backs of my legs hit the edge of the sofa. I fall back, and Belmont is on top of me. His mouth hasn't broken away from mine. Jeez, I can't think. I can only taste his tongue and the sweet chemistry of his saliva.

We moan and grunt as we kiss, kiss, and kiss some more. Our hands squeeze here and grasp for dear life there. Belmont gathers a handful of my hair and turns my head to bite down hard on my neck.

"Ah!" I gasp from the pain and pleasure.

His lips find mine again. We tumble off the sofa and onto the floor. He shoves the coffee table away, and it goes flying. Coasters and trinkets hit the carpet.

How long can we do this? The minutes tick by. His hands are more confused than his tongue and lips. He's lifting my skirt, caressing my crotch, then my butt, then my hips, then my waist, then my breasts, then my neck. Then he starts all over but not in that order.

"Shit, Daisy," he whispers.

He's back to wrapping his tongue around mine and sucking on my lips between kisses, enjoying my mouth as much as I'm enjoying his.

"Daisy," he tries again. His forehead is pinned against mine, and the sides of our noses are pressed against each other. "What the hell went wrong?"

"Everything," I whisper. "I'm sorry for what I've done."

He lifts his face, leaving my skin longing for his touch. "What have you done?" He sounds worried.

"Not what you're thinking, Belmont," I assure him. "I didn't do anything with Pete."

"You went swimming with him?"

"Yes."

"Nothing happened?"

"Well he kissed me once…"

"That fucker," Belmont glares toward the main house. "What else?"

I want to say that's it, but I want to divulge the whole truth and nothing but the truth. "Then I drowned."

"You drowned?" he roars.

"But I didn't die," I say to calm him. It does the opposite.

"What the hell, Daisy! You shouldn't have been out there without me in the first place."

"Pete's a good swimmer. He saved me."

"What?" Again, that makes him angrier.

"He had to do mouth-to-mouth resuscitation."

"Daisy…" He shakes his head. I can usually take Belmont's temperature by the density of his hard-on, and so far, it hasn't lost any of its vigor. "I hate that you chose to spend time with Pete."

"I didn't choose to. He saw me in the window and…" Jeez, I'm saying too much.

"He saw you in the window? Were you naked?"

"No," I say emphatically, and then I sigh because I still haven't told the whole truth. "He saw me topless."

"He saw your tits?" His eyebrows are severely ruffled as he lifts himself higher to search my body in the dim room.

"What are you looking for?" I ask.

He responds by tugging at the tie of my dress. He unwraps the cashmere material to expose my pink silk bra and panties. He sucks air between his teeth as he unhooks the front clamp of my bra and watches my breasts fall out. He sucks and bites the tips of my nipples. I gasp from the sting. He does it over and over and over. The longer he does it, the deeper his mouth consumes them and the harder he bites. I cry out and dig my fingers into his back. Two of his fingers slide under the crotch of my panties and inside of me.

He gasps and stares at my face. "Your tits are mine, got it?"

"Actually, they're mine, got it?" I'm only half joking.

He smirks. "I'll just have to buy them from you."

I smirk. "Name your price?"

"Daisy…" The way he says that sends my heart racing. I watch his hand dig into his pocket.

"What are you doing?" I ask anxiously.

He sets a black velvet ring box right between my breasts. "I'm going to put this right here. Don't let it drop." His naughty eyes narrow before he kisses, licks, and nibbles his way down my sternum, past my abs, then my belly.

"Oh, Jack," I sigh when he arrives at my pleasure spot.

I'm inside of his warm mouth. At first I think he's happy to be back down there because he's all over the place. He sucks one of my lower lips and then the other. He thrusts into me with his soft, hot tongue. I whimper as he works. After making me wet and soft, he latches onto my pulsating clitoris. I feel his eyes studying me in the dusky room as I suck in air and moan in my attempts to bear his all-too-consuming yet pleasurable assault. My climax is building, sparking deep inside of me. The closer it comes, the louder I get.

"Not yet," Belmont whispers thickly and stops cold turkey.

"Huh?" I'm confused. Every sensitive spot on my body has risen to the occasion.

"Just give me a minute, Daisy," he pleads. "Don't drop that box." He rests on his back beside me with his eyes closed. I know what he's doing: he's quieting his lusts. "I'm handling this all wrong." He presses the back of his arm against his eyes.

Here I am lying on the carpet with a ring box between my breasts and my panties pulled down to my thighs. I feel like I've been ravished and left to simmer in this incomplete state. "Handling what wrong?"

"You," he shouts. "You!"

"How did you want to handle me?"

He takes his arm off his eyes to dig his fingers into my vagina. I release a long breath as he presses his thumb on my clitoris and draws circles. "Not like this. You were at the wedding, weren't you?"

"The other day, yes," I moan.

"You like that, baby?" he whispers.

"I do," I confess.

"I'm going to give it to you all night, all week long, but first we have to go home. I don't want to do this here. I want you to come in our bed." He removes his hand, takes the ring box off of my chest, and puts it back in his pocket. "Say good-bye to Thelma's house."

CHAPTER 16

Found Her, Kept Her

This is it.

My mind is racing.

We left the keys to my rental car on the kitchen counter in Thelma's guesthouse. Belmont boldly returned to the table to thank Thelma for inviting him. He informed her that he's taking me home and someone will stop by in the morning to pick up the Mini Cooper and return it to the rental office. Venturing back into that room after the way we behaved... He's braver than I.

We're in Belmont's BMW. Belmont strokes my thigh, my shoulder, and then his hand wraps possessively around my neck. That's where he keeps it.

"Your skin is warm," he comments as the car stops at a sign. He pulls my mouth to his to give me a deep and passionate kiss that leaves me dizzy.

I want to say a lot, but I'm hesitant. It's probably not wise to bring up the night of that awful dinner with Adrian and Maya. "Belmont?" My word is muffled by his mouth.

"What, baby?" he breathes.

"I'm still hungry." Actually, I'm starving. I planned on eating Thelma's five-star dinner tonight. Obviously that didn't happen.

"What would you like to eat?" He's nibbling on my neck.

"Lobster rolls…" I sigh. His mouth feels so divine.

"You're so warm, babe. I missed your warm skin." He only stops nibbling on my chin when my stomach growls. "When was the last time you ate?"

"Breakfast."

"Daisy, Daisy, Daisy…" he chastises. He pulls over to the side of the road, opens the glove compartment, takes out his cell phone, and orders lobster rolls. "What else, babe?"

"Garden salad."

"Garden salad," he repeats.

"Anything else?"

"Oranges," I say for some strange reason.

"Do you have any oranges?" he asks without pause. He listens. "Just add them; I'll pay you for them." I love that my wish is his command so much that I lean over to rest my chin on his shoulder. "Yeah, sure, uh-huh. And I want it ready when I arrive in ten minutes. Thanks." He drops the phone to gather me in his arms. We make out like crazy.

"Belmont, I've been wanting to say I'm sorry." I breathe. We stop kissing. He stares longingly into my eyes. "I didn't want to make you feel dirty or ashamed of anything."

He turns his face away from me. I feast my eyes on his perfect profile. He mutters incoherently.

"Are you angry?" I ask, suddenly worried.

"No."

He slides his seat back, reaches over to guide me onto his lap, and unzips his sexy Tom Ford trousers. His penis is as hard as steel. Our mouths are parted, blowing hot air past each other's lips. He tugs the crotch of my panties aside, puts himself inside of me, and shoves my hips down on his lap. He groans with every firm thrust. He's deep, very deep inside of me. We keep our eyes connected.

I lower my mouth onto his, and he shakes his head. "No," he mutters. "I can't come—not yet. I just want to be inside of you for a minute."

Soon he takes himself out of me. I get back into my seat, and he puts his hand around my neck.

"Shit, this is frustrating," he mutters.

"What's frustrating?" I sigh. I still feel remnants of him inside of me.

"How much I want you right now. In so many goddamn ways."

I take him by the hand that's around my neck and kiss the back of it. "You can slow down, Jack. I'm not going anywhere." I smile at him.

"Promise." His gaze is delicate.

I nod.

We stop in front of a restaurant in Edgartown near the pier. I wait in the car, and he's in and out in a matter of minutes.

"Shit," he mumbles with a lopsided grin as he reaches on the floor to retrieve the cell phone. "They heard us."

I chuckle as Belmont puts the bag of food on the backseat and speeds away. He's driving really fast. I can't believe how famished I am and not solely for food. We kiss at every stop sign. His fingers have found their way to that spot under my panties. I can't believe he knows how to stimulate me and drive at the same time. I suck in air as I pin my back against the seat.

"Tell me when you're close, baby," he requests. He continues to glance at me with a watchful eye, making sure I don't forget.

"I'm close." I sigh and clamp down on his arm.

He removes his hand, cuts a sharp right, and barrels down the driveway.

We're home.

The car screeches to a stop in front of the door. Belmont hops out of the car, runs over to my side, opens the door, and guides me out. He lifts me off my feet and sits me on the warm hood. We kiss feverishly. I gasp as he shoves himself inside of me. He shifts his hips, slamming in and out of me so fast that I'm on the verge of climaxing.

"Not yet, baby..." He pulls out and pins his rigid penis against my dress. He moans before his tongue takes another quick dive into my mouth. "One day, I'm going to master this."

"Master what?" I'm barely able to say.

"Being around you without wanting to make love to you. When you walked onto the patio tonight, I wanted to rip your dress off," he says, tugging at the plush material. "Let's go to bed." He lifts me off the car and sets me on my feet.

We bring the lobster rolls, salad, and sliced oranges with us. Belmont leads me up the stairs into my old bedroom. We put the food on the dresser, and we fall onto the king-sized, comfortable bed. The mattress and bedspread feel so familiar. Instead of pillaging me right away, he spreads out beside me.

"You didn't make me feel dirty, Daisy," he says. "I knew you'd come around." He tugs the sloppy knot holding my dress closed and spreads my dress wide open. "However, I didn't think it would take that long. What the hell were you doing?"

I look at his eyes, but he's focusing on unclipping my bra. Only for a second does he glance at my eyes.

"Working, I guess. My mom wondered why in the world I cared to begin with." I skip a breath because his fingers are kneading the tip of my left nipple.

"So Heloise Krantz is your mother. I would've never guessed it." He grins. "She's a goddamn ballbuster! She fired me once before I could even finish the first sentence. She shouted, 'Get him out! Find me someone who can fucking act.' My balls were officially busted."

I chuckle. "Yeah, that sounds like her when she's working. How did you find her? And how in the world did you get her to come?"

"Your travel agent gave me her name, and I called a friend of hers. Do you know Libby Donaldson?"

"I know her," I say. She's my mother's best friend.

"First I had to tell Libby about us and what the hell I did to you, and then she called your mother, and Heloise called me. Getting her on a plane to Martha's Vineyard was the easiest part." He pauses. "She didn't even apologize for busting my balls either. And she remembered what she did."

I laugh. "Knowing my mom, she truly believes she did you a favor."

"Ha," he says. "That's what she said."

"See? I know my mom."

"She gave me her blessing." He digs that little black velvet box out of his pocket and sets it on top of the pillow. "You know what I want, don't you, Daisy?"

I take in an extremely deep, cleansing sigh. I nod.

"I know you're used to going at it alone, which is why it took you so long to leave this on my door." He slides a folded piece of paper out of his pocket and opens it. It's the note I left for him on the night of the wedding.

"Oh, you got it," I remark.

"I got it too late. Charlie was home when you left it, but he was upstairs fucking."

"Oh, you mean the young girl?"

"How do you know she was young?"

"I ran into them the day before at the coffee shop in Oak Bluffs."

"I wish I was the one who ran into you."

"I went to Linda Jeans. Two men at the counter were talking about you, I think. There were saying something about Jack being a good guy and would give one of them work."

"Did listening to them make you want me?" He lifts his eyebrows twice.

I grin. "Just as much as hearing you talk about your clean-water project and…" I look down at his pants and vest. "Is this Tom Ford you have on?"

His smile grows larger. "I thought you'd notice."

"Oh I did. And I'm so turned on."

He dips his fingers into me. "I see." He doesn't take his fingers out of me, but he doesn't shift them either.

The mere fact that he's touching me there is so erotic that all those sensitive spots tingle again.

"Oh shit, are you going to come, baby?" he asks. He's very tuned in to my body.

"I don't know," I breathe. "Maybe you should remove your fingers."

He narrows one eye to think about it. "Uh um," is his answer. "I'm going to dine on you soon, and I need you wet."

I gulp. That sounded so sexy.

"Tell me more. I need to know what you were doing when you weren't with me."

It's hard to concentrate with his fingers inside of me, but I try. "I don't know. I went to weddings, took lots of pictures."

"What for? Personal research?" He lifts his eyebrows, grinning.

"No, I changed the focus of my article. You were right; the taxicab series wouldn't work here. Did you pay Todd to drive me around?"

He chuckles. "I'm guilty."

"And what about the list?"

"What list?"

"Todd secured me a list of all the weddings that are taking place on the island. You had nothing to do with that?"

"Nope. That was all Todd. But he's a good guy like that." Belmont finally removes his fingers. "Don't move, baby." He jumps to his feet to quickly take off his vest and shirt and step out of his pants. I watch as if he's a scene in a film. His schlong is the perfect length and girth and ready to seek refuge inside of me. Once he's completely naked, he stretches, poking me in the hip with his pole. "Did you go to Emil and Sidney's wedding?"

"Um hum," I hum.

He snakes those fingers back inside of me. Once again, I skip a breath.

"You're contracting," he whispers.

"What do you mean by contracting?" I breathe.

"You're going to come…" Belmont must realize he can't stop my body from reacting to him if he's not willing to stop touching me there. He kisses and trails tender bites up my shoulder, down my collarbone, to consume my right nipple. "You're extra warm, baby, even in here." He sinks his fingers deeper.

"Maybe I still have water in my head or something. Or my body is probably healing from the trauma of drowning," I offer up as some excuse.

Suddenly he freezes. "Are you hurting anywhere?"

"No," I assure him, "I feel fine." I would be tired if I weren't so excited that he's next to me.

He guides himself down to my nether regions, and his mouth latches on to my clitoris. Belmont means to make me come and come hard. I twist and turn and clutch the bedspread. He offers no reprieve. His tongue is working so diligently that he doesn't gaze up at my face like usual.

My thighs quiver. I'm panting like crazy. It's so close. And then I'm gripped by the blast. I scream.

Belmont shoves his erection inside of me before my orgasm subsides. He grunts as he plunges in and out of me. "You're so warm and tight—and wet." He's shifting slowly, trying to delay the inevitable.

"Your body is soft all over," he mutters. "You're a goddess." He pauses. Thrusts. "I've got to have you forever." He pauses. Thrusts. "Marry me, Daisy." He pauses. Thrusts, thrusts, and thrusts again.

Did he just ask me to marry him?

"Are you asking me to marry you?"

He reaches up to grab the black velvet box. He props himself up on his elbows and opens the tiny box.

I gasp. The ring is exquisite. The larger center diamond is pink and the white diamonds surrounding it are formed into the petals of a daisy.

"I am," he replies.

"I know 'I love you' doesn't count if you're inside of me, but does that apply to 'Will you marry me?'" I ask, joking. He laughs, but I can see in his eyes that he's a little worried that I'm evading the question. "You know everyone will think we're crazy—engaged after what? Five days?"

"Six," he quickly says. "You're it for me, Daisy. If marriage isn't something you want, that's okay too, but we're going to be together either way."

"No," I say, and right away, he looks deflated. "I mean, no, I didn't want marriage before. What the hell, maybe we are crazy, but yes, I'll marry you."

He flinches, taken aback. "You'll marry me?"

"I'll marry you."

"She said yes!" he shouts victoriously. He takes the ring out of the box and slides it on my finger. "I told you your tits belong to me."

I laugh. Now that he's officially branded me, he pillages me with his rock-hard penis. He goes deep, real deep, as if he's trying to touch my soul. Sooner than later, he releases an ocean inside of me. But he doesn't pull out.

We make out feverishly, moaning and groaning until he rises again. This time, he hangs on longer. He curses and complains that he can't get deep enough.

Over the course of the night, we make love so many times that I lose count. We stop to eat, but he chooses to go down on me while I eat the lobster roll. I giggle the entire time, but we eventually get through it.

When the sun comes up, he's still filling me with his liquid fertilizer. We can't sleep. Even when the staff brings my things into the house, we're laughing and talking.

We work out some things. I'll live in Martha's Vineyard with him until February. He'll wrap up a few projects, and then we'll officially move to Tribeca for a while. I'll cancel my trip to Lima. We'll fly out to tell my parents. For some strange reason, he wants to get my father's blessing.

"You don't really need it," I try to convince him.

"Trust me, babe. I do. You said you were all wrong about your mother. If you're wrong about your father, he'll have my head if he has to walk you down the aisle without being asked to first."

"There's no walking me down the aisle. I give myself away," I say as my cell phone rings. I reach to get it before

Belmont can pull me back into his body. It's in my purse on the floor near the bed.

"It's a local number," I say and answer.

"It better not be Pete," he says as I say, "hello."

"Miss Blanchard?" a woman asks.

"Yes, this is she."

Belmont frowns. He recognizes the change my voice has taken.

"I'm calling from the Martha's Vineyard Hospital. We took some blood tests yesterday. You didn't tell us, but when was your last period?"

"Last month," I say, kind of already knowing where she's going.

"It's a little early, but you have a slightly elevated level of hCG in your blood. It's not high enough to confirm pregnancy, but we just wanted to make you aware. Why don't you come in in thirteen days and—"

"Are you sure the elevated levels aren't from swallowing contaminated water?" I hope.

"Could be, but when was the last time you engaged in intercourse?"

"Well, five minutes ago."

"What's going on?" Belmont whispers.

I lift a finger, asking him to give me a second. What she's saying sounds insane. "How can you guess it's pregnancy this soon?"

"Have you had intercourse in the last two or three days?" she asks snippily. I think I've offended her with my doubt.

"Have I had sex in the last two or three days..." I repeat absentmindedly. "Um, yeah but—"

"Well, your hCG levels increase significantly only two or three days after implantation, ma'am. So yes, the blood test can detect pregnancy, which means you can be pregnant."

"Me, pregnant?" It feels as if I'm having an out of body experience.

"Yes!" Belmont pumps his fist victoriously, but I widen my eyes in horror.

"Um, and you said re-test in thirteen days?" I ask.

He flips me on my back, takes his brand-new erection, and stuffs me with it. He takes the phone from me. "Hi, this is Belmont Lord." He pauses. "How are you, Betty?" He pauses. "Yes, I'm the father. Yes, we'll come in two weeks. How's Douglas?" He pauses. "Glad to hear it. Okay then, see you in two." He hangs up and starts thrusting me.

"What are you doing?" I stiff-arm him in the chest, but it doesn't slow his hips down.

"You're not happy?" he whispers.

He feels so good inside of me. It's messing with my clarity. "No, yes, no. We haven't even known each other for a week! I cannot be pregnant. Not this fast. Don't get your hopes up, Belmont."

He smashes his mouth on mine, kissing me greedily. "I know you are, baby. I can feel the difference. Don't worry, Daisy, having a baby isn't going to slow us down. And you won't be alone. I'll be with you every step of the way."

I sigh. "I have been hungrier than usual, but I thought it was because Thelma's always cooking. She's a great cook. But still, there may not be a baby," I caution him.

"There's a baby," he insists.

"Maybe not," I insist.

"There is."

"We'll see in two weeks."

"Until then, no more wine, but I prescribe tons of sex." I snicker. He kisses me. "I still want to know how you really feel about marrying me. Take your time and tell me the truth."

"You remember I told you that I didn't want to be married?"

"Very much so." He sighs.

"I changed my mind after talking to Sidney."

He lets out a sigh of relief. "What did she say?"

"She said that when I marry you, our souls will become one—and that's what I want." I lift my head to kiss him, and since I start, he finishes. I can hardly breathe, he kisses me so hard.

"Hey," I breathe when I'm finally able to get a word out.

"What is it?" He's smooching on my neck. Goodness, he's so dang good at that.

"What's Maya's secret? You can tell me now that we're going to be wife and husband."

"What secret?" He takes a break to ask.

"What was she doing in Las Vegas every weekend?"

"Oh," he says casually, "she was an escort."

"Like hooker escort?"

"Yes," he says. He spreads my legs, puts his face in my crotch, and commences to dine.

For the next four days, we only leave the bed to bathe in my favorite tub—where we end up having sex—and to go into the kitchen to eat—where we also end up having sex.

And this is my life now.

It's taken such a drastic change from the day I stepped foot on the island. Tomorrow, we're flying to California to get my house packed up and to officially announce our very short engagement to my parents. Belmont promised to not mention anything about the possibility of me being pregnant until it's confirmed. I'm still hoping that I'm not. Charlie didn't want to hear anything about it. Thelma did a dance once she heard. Next Thursday night, Belmont and I are joining her at the big table for a do-over. The same guests will be present, except Mandy and Pete, and we've promised to behave.

I've just finished submitting my article to Dusty. Belmont's been out most of the morning giving final instructions, or something like that, to the construction crew before our flight in the morning.

I'm packing when I feel a lump stab me in the rear end. Two familiar hands spin me around, and I'm face to face with the sexiest man on the planet.

"I've been thinking about you all morning," he croons and lifts my shirt over my head.

Yeah... his sexual appetite hasn't diminished one bit. I'm starting to think it never will. He lowers me onto the bed and, well... You know the rest.

The End

You are cordially invited

to the wedding of

Belmont Jaxson Lord

and

Daisy Louise Blanchard.

————

Be a guest in "There's Something About Her: A New York L.O.V.E. Story," the next book in the L.O.V.E. in the USA series.

℘

There's Something About Her:

A Manhattan L♡V.E Story

EXCERPT

Dear Patty Welch,

Thank you for—everything. I appreciate learning what I have under your tutelage.
I hereby resign effective immediately.

Sincerely,
Magnolia Conroy

What I really want to say is, "Thank you for teaching me that real, bona fide, mean and nasty witches exist in the world. If I ever had any doubts, well, you cured them."

I've read the letter in my hands a million times because I wrote it six months ago. One day, I'm going to hand it to Patty, walk out, and let my finances, and thereby my life, fall to pieces.

"What's going on, little Magnolia bud?" my cousin Charlie says as he flops down beside me and lifts his foot on his knee. I turn up my nose because he smells like the inside of a keg and looks like an unshaven, red-eyed hobo wearing a sloppy suit.

"Charlie," I mutter. I wish he would've chosen to sit elsewhere. I hate it when he calls me Magnolia, which he's aware of.

I prefer the flower exploding through this humongous space. My other cousin, Charlie's brother, is getting married. Belmont's bride is named Daisy-hence, the daisies.

"Why the hell did I show up for this?" Charlie grumbles as he rolls his eyes around the room, viewing it. "Goddamn daisies everywhere."

It's no secret he's in love with his brother's soon-to-be wife. But in truth, the yellow flowers aren't a bad touch at all.

We're fifty-three stories high, and this room takes up the entire floor of the building. The walls are all glass, and it's sort of like we're sitting in a garden on a perfect early evening. Inside the huge room is a makeshift duck pond near the east windows that flows into a waterfall to the south and a field of daisies rising to the north.

They wanted to take their vows against the Manhattan sunset—at 8:20 p.m. approximately—which is twenty minutes away, and that'll be at the west windows.

Twinkling white and yellow lights are tastefully placed throughout the room, and the frames of the chairs we're sitting on are made of quartz. The seat and back cushions are golden silk and patterned with little daisies.

And the guest list–it's bloated. There are at least three hundred people. Every single person looks as if they've stepped out of GQ or Elle magazine, all except me. I'm just a pale as ghost, limp-haired, overworked, underpaid, and underappreciated marketing assistant who works for the devil incarnate.

Belmont, who we call Jack, rented a cruise ship for the reception. He's given all the guests rooms to sleep off the monumental celebration he's got planned, and I'll have to skip it. My boss wouldn't give me the two days off that I requested. She wants me in the office tomorrow at six a.m. sharp to prepare for the Black Marble presentation.

The reception ship will sail tonight from the North River Pier in Manhattan to Vineyard Haven, and dock by seven p.m. tomorrow evening. Jack arranged to fly everyone back home from Martha's Vineyard. Jack said there will be lots of dancing and music by popular bands. He wouldn't tell me who they were because it's still a surprise to Daisy. He's gone gaga over this woman, but I'm not surprised. He's not the douchebag that Charlie is.

"You look like shit, Magnolia," Charlie comments, blowing his horrible breath in my face.

"Grow up, Chuck," I snap.

"No disrespect, Mags. I'm just making an observation."

"Whatever." He's such a douche.

"This is a shotgun wedding. You know she's pregnant. What a way to trap him," a very tall woman with a lot of bronze hair says in a dull, cynical tone. She's talking specifically to the freakishly thin girl who came in with her, but everyone in a five-foot radius can hear her. "How long have they known each other? Five minutes?"

That's when I realize I'm sitting with the bitter wedding day gang. I scoot to the edge of my seat to see if any empty chairs are available. There are few in the back, but I don't want to sit that far away.

Charlie, who's still slouched in his seat, leans forward to wave to the bitter woman next to me. "Mandy Hill!"

She grunts and rolls her eyes. "Great," she grumbles. "It's Charlie. You should've told your future sister-in-law to pull back on the daisies. Can you say Bridezilla?"

Now I recognize her. She's Mandy Hill, the actress. I'm waiting for Charlie to correct her. He knows the explosion of daisies was Jack's doing.

"You know, if you want to get back at him for not realizing what he lost, we can find a room and—you know…" he says instead, grinning and poking his fist back and forth.

I'm disgusted and squirm uncomfortably in my seat. This is just my luck.

"Been there, done that, doesn't work," Mandy replies to my utter shock.

Suddenly, I can't believe I'm sitting between the two of them. Thank God the full ensemble band starts. They're playing a dramatic piece that sounds like the music played during a suspenseful scene in a movie.

"Welcome to the big day!" Belmont shouts from the rear.

The entire room turns to see. In a snap, I've gone through three emotions. Dread from being sandwiched between Charlie and Mandy, curiosity from hearing Jack at the back of the room—isn't the groom supposed to be at the altar?—and now I'm smiling, enthralled by the sight of Jack holding the most gorgeous bride in the world.

"Get the hell out of here," Mandy mutters while Charlie makes a sound that's similar to a pig snorting and whips his face forward, refusing to watch the spectacle.

The wedding has officially started.

About the Author

Z.L. Arkadie (Zuleika Arkadie) is the author of the *Parched* novel series, a vampire romance with a twist, the new *L.O.V.E. in the USA* contemporary romance novel series and *The Complexities of Love and A Curse* romance serial.

She was born, raised and still to this day lives in Southern California where she enjoys the sun as well as writing, traveling and learning new things.

To learn even more about this author visit: zuleikaarkadie.wordpress.com

CPSIA information can be obtained at www.ICGtesting.com
Printed in the USA
LVOW05s1434170614

390451LV00018B/454/P

9 781491 291511